CRAZY
IN THE
COCKPIT

A RICHARD JACKSON BOOK

CRAZY
IN THE
COCKPIT

A NOVEL BY
RANDY BLUME

A DK INK BOOK

DK PUBLISHING, INC.

A Richard Jackson Book

DK Publishing, Inc.
95 Madison Avenue
New York, New York 10016

Visit us on the World Wide Web at http://www.dk.com

Library of Congress Cataloging-in-Publication Data

Blume, Randy.
Crazy in the cockpit / by Randy Blume.—1st ed.
p. cm.
ISBN 0-7894-2572-6
I. Title.
PS3552.L844C73   1999   813'.54—dc21
98-27419   CIP   AC

Book design by Dirk Kaufman
The text of this book is set in 12 point Baskerville
Printed and bound in U.S.A.

First Edition, 1999
2 4 6 8 10 9 7 5 3 1

FOR MY MOTHER,

WHO ALWAYS BELIEVED I WOULD WRITE—

EVEN WHEN I WAS TOO BUSY FLYING

CONTENTS

STALLS

I didn't know I was going to fall in love with flying during my first lesson, but I must have suspected. Because, when the editor of the college newspaper asked which reporter wanted to investigate the ad ANYONE CAN BE A PILOT FOR $20 as part of our continuing series about the truth in local advertising, I readily volunteered. And, when Dennis Sullivan, the tall, blond, baby-faced flight instructor who had been assigned by the flight school to answer my questions, insisted on proving the veracity of the slogan by offering me the opportunity to be a pilot for half an hour, I eagerly rummaged through my backpack and under the seats of my car until I came up with the requisite twenty dollars.

I told myself I was only going on the flight because I was such an open-minded reporter, but as I followed Dennis across the tarmac and diligently took notes while he unlocked the doors of a green-and-white Cessna 152, climbed up on the wing struts to peer into its fuel tanks, ran his fingers over its single propeller, and untied the ropes holding it to the ramp, I couldn't help feeling excited. I wanted to go up in that airplane.

Dennis took the right seat, and indicated that I should take the left, the pilot's seat, which, he pointed out, would be perfectly safe since the airplane was equipped with dual controls—a yoke in front of each person and two sets of pedals on the floor. Until that moment I hadn't given any thought to the concept that not everyone would consider leaving the ground in a miniature airplane with someone they'd just met (a person who, for all I knew, was not a real flight instructor but a serial killer prone to inviting unsuspecting college seniors into the sky to rape, murder, and leave them to crash while he parachuted to freedom) *safe*. Which reminded me of my only-child-of-an-overprotective-single-mother status.

"My mother would not be pleased if anything happened to me," I commented, as Dennis started the engine, listened to a stream of gibberish on the radio, and taxied us to the runway.

"The only thing that is going to happen to you," he responded, stuffing yellow earplugs into his ears, adjusting his mirrored Ray-Ban sunglasses, and fiddling with various switches and dials, "is that you're going to fall in love with flying." He gave me a broad smile, said something into the radio, and then pushed the throttle forward.

It was my first flight in anything other than an airline jet, and I was surprised at how different and thrilling it felt. The runway rushed by faster. The takeoff happened more quickly. We climbed at a steeper angle. The sky seemed closer. I reluctantly opened my notebook and tried to capture my impressions for the article.

While I was writing, Dennis announced we'd leveled off and told me to pick a bug spot on the windshield that was even with the horizon.

"A bug spot?" I asked, looking up.

"One of those gray globs," he said, pointing several out. The windshield was covered with them. "That's why they call these airplanes bug smashers. Get it?" He nudged my side with his elbow.

"Ha, ha," I said, writing down "bug smashers." My article was going to be funny. I could see the headline already: ANYONE CAN SMASH BUGS FOR $20.

"I'm serious," he said, taking the notebook and pen from my hands and tossing them into the tiny storage area behind the seats. "You've got it."

"Got what?" I asked, giving up on my notes and admiring the scenery. It was a beautiful, clear September day, and I could see all the way to the coast. I recognized the Connecticut River and wondered if I'd be able to spot the campus.

"The airplane." Dennis rested his left arm on the back of my seat and put his right hand behind his head. "You paid your money. Now you're going to be the pilot."

"You might want to put your hands back on the controls," I suggested, my initial enjoyment giving way to uneasiness. Maybe he really was crazy. "I don't know how to fly."

"This is a lesson," he said, laughing at my discomfort. "Anyway, the airplane is trimmed for level flight. Unless one of us changes something, it will stay like this until it runs out of fuel."

"How much fuel do we have?" I asked, not entirely reassured.

"About three more hours' worth," he said, assisting my reluctant hands to the control wheel. I noticed he was wearing a college ring on the third finger of his right hand. It said 1982, making him only a year ahead of me and meaning he couldn't be a very experienced flight instructor. "In order for us to stay level, all you have to do is keep your bug spot on the horizon. If you want to climb, pull back until the spot is about three inches above the horizon. If you want to descend, push forward until the spot is three inches below. Go ahead and try."

I pulled back on the controls. Gingerly. The bug spot moved above the horizon, and we climbed. I pushed forward. The bug spot moved down, and we descended. I brought it back to the horizon, and we stayed level. I even tried some turns, which worked. Naturally I'd assumed Dennis was helping, but when I glanced over I saw that his left arm was still on the back of my seat, his right hand was still behind his head, and his feet were flat on the floor, nowhere near the rudder pedals. I was flying an airplane by myself, and, I had to admit, it was amazing!

"So when are you coming for your next lesson?" Dennis asked at the end of my half hour.

"I only went up for my article," I reminded him, recovering my notebook and pen from behind the seats.

"But you fell in love with it," he said matter-of-factly. "And this month we have a special introductory rate of fifty-six dollars an hour. You'd save four dollars an hour over the regular rate."

"And how many hours does it take to get a license?" I asked, jotting down the prices.

"Forty is the FAA minimum for private pilot, though most people take closer to fifty. But solo time costs less because you're only paying for the airplane and not the instructor."

"That's almost three thousand dollars!"

"You could get a job."

"But I'm not taking flying lessons," I said, realizing the thought made me sad. "I'm writing about truth in advertising. And Anyone Can Be A Pilot For Three Thousand Dollars is a huge leap from Anyone Can Be A Pilot For Twenty Dollars."

"When you call to schedule your next lesson," he continued, ignoring both the fact that I wasn't a potential student and the notion that I was going to have to expose his flight school's ad as less than truthful, "make sure they know you want to fly with me. There are a lot of hungry flight instructors out there who would snatch you up in a minute."

Because my mother (who claimed she wanted to chronicle my career as a future Pulitzer Prize–winning journalist) subscribed to the college newspaper, there was no way for me to keep the ANYONE CAN BE A PILOT FOR $20 story from her. So I decided to preempt her inevitable hysteria by calling and explaining that, as a woman aspiring to journalistic greatness, I'd simply had no choice but to take the perfectly safe introductory flight with the highly qualified, fully FAA-licensed flight instructor in the brand new, impeccably maintained Cessna aircraft. And it had been such a fascinating experience and had given me such tremendous insight that I was convinced she would find the article thoroughly brilliant.

Which, unfortunately, did not stop my mother from entering a state of extreme consternation. Her scream through the phone could be heard all the way across the apartment, where my roommate, Karen, a premed psychology major, looked up from studying to roll her eyes. Karen had diagnosed the relationship I had with my mother as "acutely neurotic" and wanted to use it as a case study for one of her research papers.

"Have you lost your mind, Kendra Meade Davis?" my mother shrieked. "You could have been killed!"

"Sometimes a journalist has to take certain risks to get a good story," I explained.

"I never should have let you go to school so far away," she despaired. Far away was all of two hundred miles, but my mother still regarded the fact that I'd refused to apply to Princeton, where she chaired the sociology department (and where, she'd informed me on numerous occasions, I would have gotten a break on tuition and been able to live at home), as an act of defiance. "You've become so self-absorbed that you probably never even considered what my life would be like without you!"

I felt guilty enough to endure the rest of her tirade without attempting to further defend myself, but it somehow didn't seem like the right time to mention I'd already signed up for another flying lesson this week and was now searching for a job in order to pay for it.

"Stall/spin accidents are the number one cause of death for student and private pilots," Dennis announced during my fifth flying lesson, removing a comb from his back pocket, running it through his immaculately blow-dried hair, and contemplating his reflection in his Ray-Bans. "Since you can't have a spin unless a stall gets out of control, we're going to practice stalls and stall recovery until they become second nature."

I concentrated on keeping the wings level, climbing at seventy-five knots, and heading toward the practice area. In only 4.2 hours, I could start the engine, talk on the radio, taxi, take off, climb, turn, level off, descend, and, with Dennis's help on the controls, even land. So far I'd loved my flying lessons.

"Today I'm going to demonstrate a simple power-off stall," he said, reaching for the controls. I had dutifully read the section in the

Private Pilot Instruction Manual about stalls, but, although I understood the concept intellectually, I had no idea what they would feel like.

I folded my hands in my lap and removed my feet from the rudder pedals. The Cessna 152 was so small that my right thigh was resting against Dennis's left thigh, and my right shoulder was resting against his left upper arm, a situation I tended to be more aware of when I wasn't at the controls.

"First, I reduce the power," he said, bringing the throttle to idle. "Then I maintain altitude." He pulled back on the control wheel gently. "Watch the altimeter. See how we're staying level?"

I was transfixed by the nose of the airplane, which had filled the entire windshield.

"Now look at the airspeed," he continued. "What do you see?"

I forced myself to look at the airspeed indicator, which showed that the normal cruise speed of ninety-five knots had dropped to sixty and was still decreasing.

"Is this a stall?" I wasn't sure I liked this activity.

"Feel how the air is starting to burble and the wings are losing their lift?" Dennis asked, raising the nose even more. The airplane started shaking. Ominously. "That's called a buffet."

I clutched at the bottom of my seat. I definitely did *not* like this activity. It reminded me of the Cyclonic, a ride at the fair that used to come to Princeton every summer. The Cyclonic started out spinning counterclockwise, but every few minutes it would suddenly reverse direction, leaving its participants (and their stomachs) lagging a second behind. It wasn't the motion I'd disliked so much; it was the arbitrary nature of the changes and my inability to anticipate them. I was a person who liked to be in control.

"But if I just ease the yoke forward," he persisted, "we decrease the angle of attack, air flows smoothly over the wings, and the airplane flies again." He advanced the power and leveled off at our original altitude. "Now you try it."

"I think it's time to head back," I said, detaching my sweaty, trembling hands from the upholstery. "I just remembered I have a paper due tomorrow."

"According to my watch we still have twenty minutes," Dennis said, stretching his left arm across the back of my seat, moving his feet off the rudder pedals, and popping a piece of gum into his mouth. "How about some clearing turns?"

I reluctantly made turns in both directions, but I couldn't concentrate on looking for other airplanes because I was hearing, in my head, at maximum volume, my mother's voice forbidding me to perform treacherous maneuvers in an airplane whose structural integrity was unknown—an airplane that could, at any moment, shed its wings or tail, condemning me to uncontrolled impact with the ground, and thus requiring her to identify my remains with only dental records for guidance. If my death hadn't already killed her, such an exercise would surely be the final blow.

"Throttle to idle," Dennis said, placing his right hand over mine on the throttle to make sure I reduced the power. "Raise the nose to hold your altitude."

I raised the nose. Too much. We gained five hundred feet.

"Hold it here," Dennis said, cracking his gum and staring out his side window in a posture of studied nonchalance.

I held it. And held it. Until the airplane felt weightless. And totally wrong. And even worse than the Cyclonic on a bad day.

"Keep holding it," he said.

Suddenly the airplane started to shake. Not a gentle rumble like Dennis's demonstration, but a full-fledged shudder complete with the screech of the stall warning horn. Surely we were going to wind up in a spin, a violently revolving nosedive that would terminate in a spectacular fireball visible across the entire state.

"Lower the nose," Dennis suggested calmly.

I shoved the nose down. We dove.

"Level off," he said, reaching across to advance the throttle.

I brought the nose up. Way too far. We climbed a thousand feet quickly, and the airplane stalled again. I pushed the nose down, and the ground approached at an alarming rate. I closed my eyes and braced for impact.

"I've got it," Dennis said.

I felt a draft on my shoulder as he removed his arm to take over the controls and, with seemingly little effort, brought the airplane back to straight and level flight.

"We'll practice that again next time," he said.

By the middle of October I was taking two or three lessons a week and delivering pizza Sunday through Thursday nights. I had already finished the *Private Pilot Instruction Manual*, completed its accompanying workbook, and devoured any other books about flying I could find.

"You've turned this place into an obsession incarnate," Karen commented one afternoon as she moved several stacks of flying books and magazines off our sagging, found-at-the-curb-on-trash-day couch so she could sit down.

Just because I'd been building model airplanes and hanging them from the ceiling, and had plastered the walls of my room with posters of airplane cockpits, stuffed my closet with leather aviator jackets I'd found at thrift shops and yard sales, subscribed to eleven aviation magazines and newsletters, and allowed my ever-expanding collection of flying books to consume all of the floor and furniture space in our small apartment did not necessarily mean I was obsessed.

"I happen to be interested in aviation," I said, closing the newest issue of *Flying* and opening my art history book to study for tomorrow's test.

"Definition of *obsession*," Karen read from the dictionary she'd taken from the clean, organized bookshelf in her room. " 'The domination of one's thoughts or feelings by a persistent idea, image, desire, et cetera.' Ring a bell?"

"Okay," I conceded. "Maybe I'm *very* interested." And I had to admit that my schoolwork was suffering. Reading *Fate Is the Hunter* was a lot more exciting than *Silas Marner*, for example, and *Stick and Rudder* was infinitely more inspirational than the poetry of Renaissance England. "But Dennis is extremely pleased with my enthusiasm—"

"Of course he's pleased," Karen said. "The more enthusiastic you are, the more you fly. The more you fly, the more money he makes."

It was true that Dennis was rejoicing in my attendance and devotion. He was fond of shaking my hand at the end of each lesson and thanking me for being his off-season meal ticket. He called me his most dependable student and promised that if I kept up this pace, I would have my license before graduation.

On the condition that I ever learned to land, he added, as we sat in the briefing room painfully rehashing my eleventh lesson.

"The perfect landing should end in a stall just as the wheels touch the ground," Dennis said, consulting his clipboard, which listed all the mistakes I'd made that day.

"I thought we were trying to avoid stalls," I said between mouthfuls of M&Ms. Flying had a way of making me hungry, and there was a vending machine right outside the flight school.

"We're trying to avoid stalls *in the air*," he explained. "When we get back on the ground we *want* the wings to stall so they stop flying. The reason we bounced today was because you came in with too much airspeed. The airplane hit the ground, but the wings still had enough lift to fly."

In case I'd forgotten what it looked like to bounce down the runway, Dennis demonstrated with a fluorescent pink plastic airplane. I felt the actual jolts radiate through my body and settle in my head as he smashed the plastic airplane along the table—not just once or twice to illustrate his point—but seven times, a literal representation of my landing that day.

"You can stop," I said. "The wings are going to break off."

Dennis smiled in an irritatingly smug way, suggesting I'd finally gotten the point. "From now on," he said, "we're going to spend every lesson on takeoffs and landings. When you do them to my satisfaction, you can solo."

"Maybe there's a twelve-step group for flying addicts," Karen mused, spooning up filling from the spinach-and-mushroom calzone I'd made between pizza deliveries. I hadn't yet mastered the art of spinning the dough to achieve a uniform thickness, and parts of the crust were so thick we had to saw through them with a steak knife, while others were so thin the filling had oozed out.

"I'm not *addicted* to flying," I said, hacking away at a particularly stubborn piece of crust. "I'm in love with it."

"That's what alcoholics say about their booze and what drug addicts say about their heroin."

"Alcohol and drugs are dangerous," I argued, pouring tomato

sauce (which I'd brought home in a plastic cup) on the carcass of my calzone.

Karen raised her eyebrows. "And flying lessons aren't?"

"Dennis is a safe and experienced instructor," I said. "He won't let me solo until he's a hundred percent sure I'm ready."

"And when you solo, you don't pay him, right?" Karen removed the milk from the refrigerator and took a swig from the carton.

"Right," I said, putting my plate in the sink. "I just pay for the airplane."

"Better not expect to solo anytime soon," she said, finishing off the milk. "I'm sure this Dennis guy wants a little cash on hand for holiday spending."

"When am I going to solo?" I asked Dennis, who, having used telepathic powers, arrived at the airplane the very second I finished my preflight inspection. This was a feat he'd been performing since my third lesson, when he'd first sent me out to preflight without supervision.

"When you're ready," he said, climbing into the right seat. "Although I don't understand why you're in such a hurry to be rid of my handsome face and charming personality." He flashed his sanguine smile, but I couldn't get what Karen had said out of my mind.

"I already have nineteen hours," I said. "The average pilot solos in fifteen." A fact I'd picked up in my reading.

"There's no such time as *when the average person solos*," Dennis said, fitting his earplugs into his ears. "There are too many variables. Today, for instance, there's a ten-knot direct crosswind." He handed me the checklist, his indication I should start the engine.

"Is a ten-knot crosswind too strong for me to solo?"

"A ten-knot crosswind is too strong for *any* student pilot to solo," he said. "Think of what would happen to my potential for career advancement if you killed yourself up there."

I taxied toward the runway, basking in the fact that Karen was wrong and Dennis was just being vigilant, but for some reason the airplane did not want to move in a straight line.

"Where is the wind coming from?" he asked.

"Three-five-zero at one-eight," I answered, quoting the information the tower had given when I'd called for a taxi clearance.

"Then put some correction in!" Dennis grabbed his control wheel and pushed it forward, turning it all the way to the left. "Do you want us to wind up in a ditch?"

"Sorry," I said meekly.

"I think it would be best for me to demonstrate the first crosswind takeoff and landing," he said.

I relinquished the controls and sat back in my seat.

Dennis put in the proper crosswind correction during takeoff so the airplane never strayed from the centerline. Then he corrected for the strong wind aloft by crabbing so the airplane's track over the ground was exactly half a mile from the runway at all times. And then he made a flawless crosswind landing.

"I'm ready to try it now," I said, after his fourth takeoff. Dennis's skill was certainly impressive, but I kept hearing Karen's voice reminding me that I wasn't paying to be impressed.

"Don't you want to see one more landing?" he asked, holding the controls lovingly.

"No, thanks."

I took over, and Dennis removed a mechanical pencil from his pocket and flipped to a clean page on his clipboard. We were on the downwind leg of the traffic pattern, and I knew the wind was coming from the right. Therefore, I would have to point the nose of the airplane to the right to avoid being blown too close to the runway. No problem.

But I must not have corrected enough, because I flew across the final approach course at a forty-five-degree angle to the runway.

"Go around," Dennis said, writing on his clipboard.

In the second pattern I concentrated so hard on correcting for the wind, I forgot to descend. We wound up over the runway threshold still at a thousand feet.

"Go around," Dennis said, writing on his clipboard.

The third pattern was just right until I tried to make a normal landing. I pointed the nose straight down the runway, but the crosswind blew us over the grass.

"Go around," Dennis said, writing on his clipboard.

On the sixth go-around the tower asked if we were all right.

"Just getting a little crosswind experience," Dennis told them, writing on his clipboard.

"This time it's going to be perfect," I said. I'd already made every mistake in the book; there was nothing else I could do wrong.

"I hope so," Dennis answered. "I'm running out of paper."

Amazingly enough, I flew an adequate pattern and made a decent landing.

"Let's see if you can do it again," he said.

I did it again.

"Once more."

I did it once more.

"That wasn't bad when you finally decided to put the airplane on the ground," Dennis grudgingly allowed as we taxied in.

∞

On the Tuesday before Thanksgiving, my mother called as I was getting ready to go to the airport for my last lesson before heading down to New Jersey early the next morning.

"I've decided to do Thanksgiving myself this year," she said.

"Really?" I asked. My mother was the queen of takeout. I seriously doubted her oven had been turned on since I'd left for college.

"I've made lists of everything that needs to be done, but I could use your help. If you left right now, you could be home by five."

"I can't leave right now," I said.

"Why not? You don't have classes on Tuesday afternoons." Which my mother knew because she had a copy of my class schedule.

"But I have a lot of other . . . stuff . . . to do." Since my mother's reaction to my first flight had been less than encouraging, I'd never quite gotten around to telling her about my pursuit of a private pilot's license.

"Bring your homework home," she suggested. "You'll have all weekend to work on it."

"Well, I have . . . um . . . plans . . ." I stammered.

"Ah, *plans*," she said, pausing. "Then I guess I'll do what I can without you. Do these *plans* have a name?"

"I'm sort of in a hurry. I'll tell you all about him tomorrow." I grabbed my backpack with my flying gear and ran out the door. My mother thought I had a date. Well, that was okay. The dating concept could work very well. It would explain why I was out most nights, why I was behind in all my classes, and why I'd only completed two graduate school applications. Plus it would allow me to be private and secretive. Even my mother drew the line somewhere, and that somewhere was men. She'd seldom asked me anything about my social life, and she'd rarely told me anything about hers.

∞

Over the past week, it had been either too cloudy, too windy, snowing, or raining every time I'd been scheduled for a lesson. Today was clear and balmy, though, and I was ecstatic to be back in the airplane. The wind sock, I noticed as I did my preflight, was completely limp. With no wind, maybe I would make some good landings.

But, to my dismay, Dennis insisted we fly out to the practice area to work on stalls.

"You haven't flown in a week," he said, pencil and clipboard in hand. "I want to make sure you remember everything."

I spent half an hour doing stalls, but Dennis found something wrong with all of them. I either gained too much altitude, strayed too far from the original heading, recovered before the airplane actually stalled, or was simply not smooth enough.

"We're not going back to the traffic pattern until you get them right," he said.

I did four more stalls, but they weren't good enough either.

"I'm in no hurry," he said, cleaning his sunglasses with a special cloth he kept in the pocket of the leather jacket he'd taken to wearing since the weather had gotten cooler. "It's a nice day, and I'm up here logging hours and making money—"

"Well, I've had it with stalls!" I exploded, turning the airplane back toward the airport without asking Dennis. Logging hours and making money! He didn't care about teaching me to fly at all! It was only about what I could do for him. "And I've had it with your patronizing, condescending—"

"I'm tired of stalls, too," he broke in. "But I can't let you solo until I'm sure—"

"—I won't ruin your career," I finished, tuning the radio to the tower frequency. I called in our position as ten miles south of the airport, and the controller cleared us to enter a left downwind for runway two-zero. "Well, you can find yourself another way to log hours and make money because I'm done flying with you!"

"The logging hours and making money thing was a joke," he said.

"It wasn't funny," I said, entering the traffic pattern. Abeam the end of the runway, I reduced the power and lowered the flaps ten degrees.

"Then I apologize," Dennis said.

"It's too late," I said, lining up on final approach and lowering the flaps all the way. I'd already spent fourteen hundred dollars on over twenty-five hours of instruction. And it was all a waste. Dennis was never going to let me solo. I would never get my license if I kept flying with him.

My landing was a greaser, a touchdown characterized by only the subtlest squeak of the tires.

"Taxi over to the tower," Dennis said, zipping up his jacket.

"What for?"

"So I can get out."

"Why are you getting out?" All kinds of bizarre thoughts were going through my mind. Maybe he had to go to the bathroom and couldn't wait until we taxied back to the flight school, but that was silly, because the flight school wasn't any farther away than the tower. Maybe we'd done something wrong, and he was going to apologize to the air traffic controllers, but he could do that by phone or even walk over after we shut the airplane down. Maybe he was so tired of me he was going to walk away right now.

He unfastened his seat belt and smiled, and realization suddenly dawned—Dennis was getting out because I was going to solo.

"Oh, no," I said, becoming very cold inside. "This is not a good idea. In fact, this is a crazy idea. I'm sorry I thought you weren't a good instructor. You're a great instructor." I was starting to panic. "And you're perfectly right that I'm not ready to solo. I can't even do stalls. Twenty-five hours isn't really a lot of time. I think I need another five hours before I solo. Maybe even ten . . ."

"Do three full-stop landings and come pick me up," he said, opening his door and jumping down onto the tarmac. "I'll be watching you from upstairs."

Dennis walked over to the tower, opened the door, and disappeared inside. I was alone in the airplane, which seemed huge without him. I couldn't seem to catch my breath. I couldn't stop shaking. I felt like I might either faint or throw up. I had to get out of the airplane fast, or something terrible was going to happen!

But I couldn't remember how to shut down the engine. I couldn't leave an airplane with a spinning propeller sitting on the ramp. It wasn't safe. It probably wasn't even legal. The checklist. I just needed the checklist. There it was, right on Dennis's empty seat. I would complete the "Engine Shutdown" portion, then run for the parking lot. My mother was right; I had been out of my mind to take flying lessons. I would find another safer, cheaper hobby—like quilt making or basket weaving. I would quit my pizza delivery job, concentrate on my classes, write more articles for the newspaper, and finish my graduate school applications. I wouldn't miss flying at all. Not one little bit.

I picked up the checklist, and it was suddenly easier to breathe. I wasn't quite as dizzy. I took several deep breaths. I was still shaking, but instead of shutting down the engine, I began to read the "Before Takeoff" section.

∞

Although Karen had bet twenty dollars I wouldn't be able to contain what she called my "excessive postsolo exuberance" successfully enough to get through Thanksgiving without mentioning anything about my flying lessons, it turned out my mother wouldn't have noticed if I'd flown an airplane through the living room. She was too busy with Norman, her new boyfriend, who I found comfortably ensconced in our town house.

Under normal circumstances I would have been shocked and furious that the den had been made into Norman's office, that the hall bathroom—my bathroom—had been stripped of its Laura Ashley wallpaper, painted dark green, and given to Norman (although my mother had saved my things in a white wicker basket, which she insisted would be easy to carry to and from the bathroom when I visited), and that she had neglected to mention either Norman or the renovations in any of our phone conversations. Especially since my mother had always told me men were fine for dating, but she could never *live* with one because their smelly socks alone could contaminate the entire house.

But these weren't normal circumstances. Graduate schools were going to be looking at this semester's grades, and if I didn't get three papers written and several hundred pages read, I might not even pass all my classes. So I was glad that my mother was busy with Norman, that Karen hadn't let me bring home any distracting flying books, and that I was able to spend the weekend locked in my room catching up.

There were only three weeks between Thanksgiving and the end of the semester, and although the weather was never good enough to solo again, I did get in a few more lessons. Three hours of night flying were required for the private pilot's license, and Dennis suggested we get them out of the way while the days were short.

I didn't see night flying as something to get out of the way. It sounded exciting to me. I'd finally get to see all those colored lights I'd learned about—blue for taxiways, white for runways, alternating white and green to designate an airport, red position light on the left side of the airplane, green on the right.

"You're not going on a date," Karen said, looking up from the notes she was studying while I tried on everything in my closet.

"I'm just trying to find something comfortable." I was debating between my blue and black jeans. The black jeans were tighter and more flattering, but the blue jeans looked better with the soft white sweater I'd decided to wear.

"Sweatpants are *comfortable*." Karen wore sweatpants all the time.

I settled on the black jeans and began tackling the outer garment decision. My favorite leather jacket, the one I'd found at the Salvation Army store next to the pizzeria, was beat up enough to look authentic, but it also had holes in the leather, a ripped lining, and wasn't designed for temperatures in the low teens. My other leather jackets were in even worse shape, and my down parka, though certainly warm enough, made me look like an overinflated balloon.

"Since when do you care how you look for your flying lessons?" Karen asked, highlighting half a page in her cell biology textbook. "I thought your instructor was a supercilious, narcissistic opportunist."

I hadn't seen Dennis since my solo, but I'd found myself reliving the hug he'd given me on more occasions than I was willing to admit. He'd congratulated me as soon as I picked him up at the tower, but it wasn't until the airplane had been tied down and we were alone in the briefing room that he'd put his arms around me.

"No hard feelings?" he'd asked, pressing me against his leather jacket.

"About what?" I'd been so surprised by his demonstration of affection, I hadn't even known what he was referring to.

"Nothing," Dennis had said, squeezing me tighter. "Nothing at all."

"There are good things and bad things about night flying," Dennis lectured, as I leveled off at three thousand feet. "Traffic is much easier to see, and there's usually less of it. The controllers tend to be more relaxed and friendly. But, if the engine quits, your only sure bet for landing is a lighted airport. You can't rely on an open field at night."

After three months of flying with Dennis, I should have recognized a hint when I heard one. But I was too busy trying not to shiver. I had chosen the leather jacket with the ripped lining, and I was absolutely freezing.

Suddenly the engine quit.

Remain calm, I told myself. I'd practiced engine failures many times. Of course, it had always been during daylight, and I'd always been able to find a suitable field for a potential landing, but the procedure was the same at night.

"Set up best glide speed," I said aloud. "Then look for a place to land." It would have been nice if I'd been paying enough attention to remember where the nearest airport was, but at least I knew the direction in which we'd been heading and that Meriden Airport was somewhere out there.

"Next, apply carburetor heat," I continued. "Then check the mixture." The mixture was full rich, but Dennis, it turned out, had pulled the throttle back to idle and was now looking out his window and whistling what sounded like the song from *An Officer and a Gentleman*. I started to push the throttle forward again, as if it were a real emergency, but his hand covered mine so I wouldn't be able to. I'd certainly felt Dennis's hands on mine before—he always seemed to be correcting something I was doing wrong—but this was the first time I noticed how warm and soft they were.

I reminded myself to concentrate and kept searching for Meriden's rotating beacon. Finally I saw it off in the distance. But we were already down to eighteen hundred feet and sinking rapidly. Even I could tell we weren't going to make it. My shivering had given way to sweat.

"So what are we going to do?" Dennis asked, clearing the throttle so we wouldn't end up with an authentic engine failure.

I stared out the window at the ground. Dennis was right—there was no way to distinguish a field from a forest at night. But I did see a highway.

"We're going for the highway," I said, lining up with the traffic.

"Good," he said, restoring the engine and putting his arm across my seat. "Take us back to Hartford now. We'll practice some night landings."

I hadn't realized I'd been sitting on the edge of my seat, but now that the crisis was over, I could lean back and relax. Relax against Dennis's arm. Something I surely must have done a hundred times— since he'd always insisted that this was the only comfortable position for his long limbs—but something that, until now, I'd never thought about before.

"It's so beautiful at night," I observed. The radio was quiet, and the view of multicolored twinkling lights was breathtaking. "And so romantic." I held my breath, waiting to see how Dennis would react to my opening. He was, after all, the one who had started all this with his hug.

"I suppose," he said. "If you want to be here."

"There's somewhere else you'd rather be than with your most dependable student?" I asked, hoping he'd smile and tighten his arm around my shoulders.

"I just get frustrated not being able to fly," Dennis said.

"What do you call this?"

"This isn't flying," he said. "It's teaching."

"Excuse me for contributing to your misery," I said, wishing I'd worn my warm parka. Why had I bothered dressing up for Dennis? What had gotten into me? "I was under the mistaken impression that you *enjoyed* flight instructing."

Dennis sighed. "You don't understand this business," he said. "I want to fly for the airlines. But the only way to get an airline job is with a few thousand hours, preferably multiengine hours. The best way to get multiengine hours is to get hired by a commuter airline. The only way to get hired by a commuter airline is to have charter experience. The way to get charter experience is to flight instruct at a school that has a charter department until the chief pilot notices you exist. In order to get the chief pilot to notice you exist, you have to work all the time, including nights and weekends."

"Then you should be grateful to me for providing you with the opportunity to work nights," I said.

"I am grateful to you, Kendra." He smiled, coming out of his funk. "You're a real trouper to put up with me. But, on the other hand," he continued, squeezing my shoulder affectionately, "you'll never find another flight instructor with my great looks and extraordinary pilot skills."

∞

Before leaving for Christmas vacation, Karen and I strategized about whether or not to tell my mother I'd been taking flying lessons. Karen's fear was that my mother wouldn't let me come back for my last semester, leaving her without both her best friend and her roommate. But I was tired of having to keep my lessons to myself, and since I'd planned to bring my flying books with me to Key West (where my mother rented a condominium every Christmas) in order to study for the private pilot written exam, I chose to adopt the policy of reading what I wanted and, if asked, tell all.

But no one asked. My mother and Norman got up early every morning to bike, snorkel, or sail, and I sat by the pool with my books and Jennifer, Norman's sullen twelve-year-old daughter, who was angry because she'd been dragged away from her friends in Phoenix to a place that didn't even have a decent mall.

In January I started cross-countries, flights to other airports. Each trip required several hours of preflight planning—marking routes and checkpoints on aeronautical charts; measuring magnetic course and distance between checkpoints; calling the flight service station for weather briefings; and computing headings and ground speeds based on winds aloft—and I loved every minute of it. Unlike stalls, cross-country flying had a purpose: to get from one airport to another. I finally felt like I was on my way to becoming a real pilot.

"Where are we?" Dennis asked. It was my second cross-country, and we were en route to Poughkeepsie, New York.

I checked my flight log. Although I'd marked the time over the last checkpoint, the intersection of a highway and a power line, we were overdue at the next checkpoint, a small lake. I looked out the window and saw houses, farms, and trees. I then consulted my aeronautical chart, which depicted neither houses, farms, nor trees.

"About here," I answered, pointing to a vague area on the chart.

"About here," Dennis repeated, studying the area I'd pointed to. "Have we passed New Preston yet?"

"Um . . ." I looked for New Preston on the chart. It was a tiny town defined by two highways and a lake. "Not yet," I said, taking a wild guess.

"Let me know when we do," Dennis said. He yawned, slid down in his seat, and closed his eyes.

I stared out the window, hoping we'd fly over something identifiable. This cross-country was not turning out to be nearly as much fun as the first one, when Dennis had pointed out checkpoints, shown me how to keep a flight log, and talked about some of the charters he'd copiloted on over the holidays.

After fifteen minutes of nothing but farms and trees, I was rewarded with the sight of an airport. A medium-sized airport with intersecting runways and a control tower. Now, at least, I'd be able to figure out where we were. I pulled out the chart and skimmed our route of flight for airports with intersecting runways. There was Danbury, about twenty miles south of our course. There was Westchester, about fifty miles south. And, there was Stewart, about fifteen miles beyond Poughkeepsie. Great. We were totally lost.

"I think we might be slightly off course," I announced to Dennis, hoping he'd be pleased with my use of understatement.

He opened his eyes. "You *think?*"

"We're definitely off course," I said.

"Well, get us back *on* course."

"I can't," I said. "We're lost."

"Lost?" he asked, widening his eyes. "How could we be lost?"

"I missed a few checkpoints," I admitted. "If you could just tell me where we are, I'd be able to get us to Poughkeepsie.

"I don't know where we are," he said. "I'm just a passenger."

"Come on, Dennis," I pleaded. "This is only my second cross-country."

"Do you think flying is a game?" he asked. "Do you think you can stop playing any time you feel like it?"

"What are you talking about?" I asked.

"I'm talking about signing you off for solo cross-countries, I'm talking about your navigational skills. About your judgment. About your ability to cope with stress."

"I didn't know this was a test," I said.

"Every lesson is a test for the times you're out there alone," Dennis said. "When there's no one else to take over. When giving up means tragedy."

"Okay, you've made your point," I said. "What do you want me to do now?"

"I want you to take me to Poughkeepsie," he said.

"I suppose I could try using the VOR," I said. The VOR was a navigational radio. Dennis had explained its use, but I had never tried it.

"That sounds like an excellent idea," he said, leaning back in his seat. "Wake me up when we get there."

On the night before my first solo cross-country, I stayed up until two in the morning planning and replanning my route of flight from Hartford to Keene, New Hampshire. I'd already been there once with Dennis, and it was a fairly easy route, but I wanted to make sure everything was exactly right.

"It all looks good to me," Dennis said, checking my flight log the next morning. "Make sure someone signs your logbook in Keene so I know you really landed there."

"What about the weather?" I asked, half hoping it wasn't good enough. "The forecast is calling for ceilings of ten thousand feet by noon."

"You won't be flying above fifty-five hundred feet," Dennis said.

"Maybe February isn't the best month for solo cross-countries," I said. "The weather could be very unstable—"

"Good-bye, Kendra," Dennis interrupted, heading into the briefing room to meet another student. "I'll see you when you get back."

I gathered up my papers and the key to the airplane and walked out to the ramp, trying not to think about all the terrible things that could happen. Such as flying into a cloud and winding up in a graveyard spiral. Or flying into military airspace and getting shot down. Or landing at the wrong airport. Or having an engine failure.

I performed the most thorough preflight in the history of aviation and took my time organizing my charts, flight logs, and pencils so they would be within easy reach. I called the flight service station on the radio for another weather briefing, but the reports hadn't changed. Finally, I had no choice but to go.

The first few checkpoints passed underneath exactly where they were supposed to be, so I knew the winds aloft forecast was accurate and my heading was correct. I marked down my times abeam Westover Air Force Base and the Quabbin Reservoir Dam and computed my ground speed. I was just starting to feel that I might actually make it to Keene when I flew into a blizzard.

Snow swirled outside all the windows, restricting my view of the ground. Do not panic, I told myself. This is similar to flying into a cloud. And the procedure for flying out of a cloud is to use the instruments to make a one-hundred-and-eighty-degree turn. Since my heading was twenty degrees, all I had to do was turn until the heading indicator read two hundred degrees, and I would fly back into the clear air I had come from.

I rolled the airplane into a shallow right bank and watched the numbers increase on the heading indicator. I'd been only two checkpoints away from Keene, and now I'd have to fly back to Hartford without landing. And if I didn't *land* at Keene, the flight wouldn't count as a solo cross-country. Which would be a total waste! And it was all Dennis's fault. He should have known that lowering ceilings could present a problem. But he'd sent me out anyway. Since I was flying solo and only paying for the airplane, he didn't seem to care what happened to me.

Halfway through my turn, the snow stopped. The ground appeared below, and I saw that I was over Orange Airport, one of my checkpoints. I rolled into a left turn and picked up my original heading. It was clear in that direction, too. Except for a few white patches on the ground, the snowstorm might never have happened. I marked the time on my flight log and continued on to Keene.

On my first night home for spring break, my mother announced we were going out for dinner, which, given her lack of interest in cooking, wasn't especially unusual. But then she ordered champagne, which was unusual (she was a red wine drinker). She and Norman kept looking at each other and smiling, and I figured they were going to tell me they were getting married. Last semester I might have been upset, but now I was starting to realize I liked having the focus of my mother's attention on someone else.

But when the champagne was poured and my mother and Norman raised their glasses, it seemed they were toasting me.

"I know the official letter hasn't come yet," my mother began. "But a little birdie from the registrar's office who knows another little birdie in New York gave me the good news today—you got into the Columbia School of Journalism! Isn't that wonderful? You'll be able to come home for weekends, and I'll be able to visit whenever I'm in the city. In fact, Norman and I were thinking about getting a little place in the Village."

I raised my glass and forced myself to smile. I'd been so caught up with flying and classes (all of which I needed to pass in order to graduate) that I'd put graduate school on the back burner. And, until this moment, I hadn't realized how much I'd been hoping I wouldn't get in anywhere. Because then I would have had an excuse to pursue an entirely different field. Like aviation.

My mother and Norman went on discussing the merits of living in New York, and I impulsively decided this was as good a time as any to tell them about my piloting pursuit.

"At least I'll be close to Teterboro," I mentioned casually, "so I can keep up with my flying."

"Your mother mentioned something about flying back in the fall," Norman said. "It's good to have a specialty in journalism, and I'm sure there aren't many women writing about aviation."

"She only went on one flight," my mother said. "That hardly makes her an authority. Anyway, I think she should stick with features, where she's demonstrated genuine talent."

"It's been a few flights," I said sheepishly. "I've even soloed."

My mother grabbed Norman's arm, and for a moment I thought she was going to let loose with one of her colossal screams. But Norman spoke first.

"Congratulations," he said, pouring more champagne. "This is a double celebration, then."

I smiled gratefully at him and downed my glass of champagne.

"I hardly see that a daughter flagrantly defying her mother is a cause for celebration," my mother commented, pushing her champagne glass away. "But my friends warned me this would happen someday. They always said Kendra and I shared too intense a bond. That it would be impossible for me to bring anyone else into our relationship. This betrayal is her way of punishing me for you, Norman."

"You can't blame her entirely, Rachel," Norman said, taking her hand. "You kept saying you were going to tell her about us, but she didn't find out until she came home and found me in the house. You haven't set the best example, you know."

But instead of giving Norman a piece of her mind as I expected (based on past experience), my mother simply smiled at him, touched his face where it looked like he'd cut himself shaving, and blandly told me she hoped we wouldn't keep secrets from each other again.

In April, after I had completed the required twenty hours of solo flight time, Dennis and I started reviewing for my checkride, the flight with an FAA examiner that would (I hoped) yield my private pilot's certificate.

"How long have we been practicing stalls, Kendra?" he asked in the classroom after our first review session.

"Since September."

"Eight months. You should be able to show me a decent stall by now."

"I tried." My stalls hadn't been that bad. On the takeoff/departure stall I'd gained about a thousand feet, but I'd gotten back to our original altitude as soon as I'd recovered. On the approach/landing stall my heading had been a little off, but I'd corrected that in the recovery, too. As far as the accelerated stall went—well, I'd never liked steep turns to begin with. So I'd recovered a little early, before the buffet. But it wasn't like I didn't know the procedure.

"You could have fooled me." He shook his head with exasperation. "I want you to go up and practice stalls by yourself for at least three hours. You can schedule with me again next week."

"But I already finished my solo hours," I protested.

Dennis was silent for a few minutes, seeming to study a teaching mock-up of a Cessna 152's instrument panel. "You'll never get your license with that attitude," he finally said, turning to face me.

"What attitude?"

"Why *are* you trying to get your license?" he asked.

"I'm in love with flying," I said, attempting to lighten the conversation. "Just like you predicted on my first flight."

"It doesn't look that way to me," Dennis said. "You hate soloing. You don't want to practice. You're afraid of stalls and spins and getting lost and everything else. So what, exactly, are you in love with?"

"I love the feeling I have when I fly," I said. "It's like being more alive. Colors are brighter, the air is clearer, and I'm more in control . . . I don't know how to explain it."

Dennis paced back and forth in front of the chalkboard. "Maybe we're going about this wrong," he said. "If it's only the *feeling* of flying you love, maybe you could skip the whole license thing and just go up with an instructor now and then. I'd be happy to do that with you."

"I thought you understood," I said in despair. "I thought *you* felt the same way."

"I'm trying to understand," he said. "But what I see is a girl who's spent close to three thousand dollars attempting to add a little excitement to her last year at college. I've enjoyed working with you, Kendra, but you're just not where you should be at this point. My advice is to stop wasting your money and find yourself another hobby."

"But I want to be a flight instructor," I blurted out, surprising myself as much as Dennis, who opened his mouth and stared at me for a full minute before laughing.

"A flight instructor?" he asked. "You?"

"Yes, *me*." Although I'd sent in my deposit to Columbia, and although my mother had already started asking her little birdies to keep their eyes and ears open for student apartments in decent buildings, I got depressed whenever I thought about graduate school. What I really wanted to do was fly. "And I'm going to get my license," I told Dennis, with more resolve than I'd known I possessed. "So if you won't help me, I'll find another instructor who will!" I stood up, grabbed my backpack, and walked to the door before I lost my nerve and started to cry.

"Wait," Dennis said, reaching for my arm and pulling me back to the table. "I didn't realize it was so important to you." He brushed away my hair, which had fallen into my face, and looked into my eyes. "Now that I know how serious you are, we'll keep plugging away until you can put it all together."

"The problem with Dennis is that he doesn't take me seriously as a pilot," I told Karen, who had wandered into the kitchen after an all-night study session.

"I didn't know you wanted him to take you seriously as a pilot," Karen said, rubbing her eyes and pouring herself a mug of coffee. "I thought you wanted him to take you seriously as a *woman*."

"That was only briefly," I said, turning on the typewriter and inserting a piece of paper. I had a twenty-page paper due on Monday, which I hadn't yet started. "When I told him I wanted to be a flight instructor, he laughed. He thought I was joking."

"Why did you tell him you wanted to be a flight instructor?" Karen asked, sitting down with her coffee at the rickety kitchen table that also served as my desk.

"Because it's what I want to do," I answered, typing my name at the top of the page.

"In addition to graduate school?" she asked.

"*Instead* of graduate school," I said, typing the title of my paper: "Images of Flight in Contemporary Women's Poetry."

"It's the end of the semester," Karen said, draining her mug. "You're under a lot of pressure. You haven't told your mother that you don't want to go to graduate school, have you?"

"Of course not," I said.

"And you haven't said anything to Columbia yet?" she continued.

"No."

"Then your life is still salvageable."

The lesson had gone well, I thought. I'd performed every maneuver required for the private pilot checkride, and Dennis hadn't uttered a word of criticism. In fact, he hadn't uttered a word, period. For all the company he'd been, I might as well have been flying alone and saving the instructor fee.

"Do you have a few minutes?" he asked as we walked across the ramp toward the flight school. "I'd like to talk to you."

"This sounds serious," I said, wondering if maybe I'd been wrong and the lesson had actually gone so poorly Dennis was going to prohibit me from ever flying again.

"It's nothing bad," he said, smiling reassuringly. "We can even sit outside if you want to."

It was warm and sunny, and I was happy to sit down on a bench outside the flight school. Even though it was noisy when an airplane started up on the ramp, it was better than the stuffy, windowless classroom.

"Let's see," he began, sitting next to me and consulting his clipboard. "Slow flight, steep turns, and ground reference maneuvers were all within tolerances. Cross-country flight planning and navigation were fine. On the short-field landings, don't worry about being smooth, the idea is to land in the shortest distance possible. That usually means you hit a little harder, but it's better than rolling off the end of the runway."

"Okay," I said, trying to pay attention but wondering what it really was Dennis wanted to talk about.

"Stalls," Dennis continued, pausing to ponder his notes. "What can I say about your stalls?"

There were numerous things Dennis had said about my stalls in the past, and none of them had been good. I prepared myself for the worst.

"Well, your stalls were all right."

"*All right?*" I asked, incredulous. "As in, nothing was wrong with them?"

"They won't keep you from your certificate," he said. "Listen, I know we're scheduled for one more lesson before your checkride, but I'm going to go ahead and sign you off today."

"You're signing me off *early?*" This was getting more unbelievable by the minute. "The person you advised to find another hobby?"

"I was wrong about that," Dennis said, turning to face me. I could see my reflection in his sunglasses. "The thing is—well, I got a job with a commuter airline, and I leave tomorrow. You could take a lesson or two with another instructor, but I really think you're ready."

"You mean you won't be here for my checkride?" It wasn't so much that I was going to miss Dennis. We would only have had one more lesson together anyway. It was just that without him on hand to witness my triumph (because I saw, with absolute clarity, that I would easily pass the checkride), no one would really care. Certainly not my mother, who hadn't said a word about my flying lessons since our one and only conversation over spring break. And certainly not Karen, who would be happy because she knew how important my private pilot's license was to me, but who still, deep down, considered flying to be a waste of my intelligence.

"No, I'll be in Bangor flying a twin-engine turboprop." Dennis was so excited he could hardly sit still.

"Congratulations," I said with more enthusiasm than I felt.

"So, do you have your logbook?"

I pulled my logbook out of my backpack and handed it to Dennis. As he wrote and babbled on about base assignments and uniform costs, I suddenly felt very lonely.

"Make sure and let me know how the checkride goes," he said, returning my logbook. "If I can document ten successes within two years, my flight instructor certificate will be renewed automatically."

"I'll probably never see you again," I observed. In three weeks I'd be graduating and going home to my summer job of teaching tennis. And, although I hadn't told my mother yet, at the end of the summer I'd be moving to San Francisco with Karen. She'd be going to medical school at UCSF, and I'd be enrolling in flight school in Oakland.

"Sure you will," he said. As if from a distance I saw him put his arm across my shoulder and hug me to his chest. But I couldn't feel anything. Not the sun or the wind or the absence of warmth when he let go. "Give me a year in Maine, and then start looking for me in the cockpit of a 727."

Dennis stood, picked up his clipboard and pen, and opened the door to the flight school. He looked back to see if I was following, but I decided to stay on the bench a little longer and watch the airplanes take off and land.

SPINS

H ow could this have hap-
pened?" my mother wailed
when I'd told her I was defer-
ring graduate school to
become a professional pilot. "I sent you to the best schools. I took
you to museums, concerts, the theater. I kept the house filled with
books. I didn't let you watch TV or eat Twinkies. I don't understand
it. Where did I go wrong?"

"You didn't go wrong," I'd said. "I had a wonderful childhood
and a great education. But I love to fly. And you always told me I
should do what I love."

"I meant writing. Or academics. Or even law or medicine," she'd
lamented. "Not this—this Greyhound Driving of the Skies. What will
I tell my friends?"

"You can tell them that I wanted a year off before graduate

school, and that I'm living in San Francisco, taking courses, and doing some teaching," I'd said.

Which was what had happened. Karen and I had driven to California over Labor Day weekend and moved into an apartment in Haight-Ashbury. She'd begun medical school orientation, and I'd enrolled at the California Aeronautics Academy in Oakland, where I was working toward my commercial, instrument, multiengine, and flight instructor ratings. And, since I had passed all the FAA written exams in my first month at the academy, and because I was the only student whose native language was English (not to mention the only American student, the only woman student, and the only college graduate—information I neglected, for obvious reasons, to share with my mother), the director of ground training had offered me a job (at five dollars per hour) tutoring my fellow students, for whom academics posed a greater challenge.

Such as Ahmed, my current, to borrow Dennis's term, meal ticket.

"I offer you two hundred dollars," Ahmed said, scratching his fat stomach and jangling the thirty gold chains he wore around his neck. The chains seemed to be some sort of status symbol, and Ahmed was very conscious of status.

"You'll still have to take the test," I answered. Ahmed had already failed his private pilot written exam four times, and his family had permitted him only one more chance before recalling him home to Saudi Arabia in disgrace.

"Okay," he said, undaunted. "Five hundred dollars for you to take the test for me."

"I can't do that, Ahmed."

"Why not? You're smart. You know the answers they want."

"They check IDs."

"Okay, okay," Ahmed said, thinking about it. "One thousand dollars to teach me the right answers."

"That's what I'm trying to do."

"I *have* to pass the test," Ahmed said.

"Then you *have* to study." Every session Ahmed attempted to bribe me, and every session I refused—although I certainly could have used the money. Whereas my mother had fully and happily intended to pay for graduate school, she had refused to pay for any of my flight training, claiming that supporting my "flying habit" would be akin (due to its "self-destructiveness") to supporting a cocaine habit. So I waitressed four nights a week and tutored whenever I could. "Did you do the practice test I gave you yesterday?"

"Right here," he said, pulling a crumpled answer sheet out of his black vinyl flight bag. The bag was liberally adorned with stickers of various airplanes, which I'd learned was another status symbol.

I examined Ahmed's answer sheet. It had been a twenty-question test, and twenty circles were filled in. The first ten were done neatly in blue ink, and I knew they would be correct because Ahmed had obviously paid someone else to do them. Ahmed himself used only black ink (blue ink, he claimed, looked cheap). The last ten questions were done in black ink. There were numerous smudges and cross-outs, as if Ahmed had carefully considered his answers. But when I laid my answer key on top, only one of the black answers (yet all of the blue answers) was correct.

"That's fifty-five percent, Ahmed," I said, handing back his graded test.

"Not bad," he said. "It's better than half, right?"

"The FAA minimum passing grade is seventy percent."

"Okay," Ahmed said, raising his pudgy arms in resignation.

"I give you two thousand dollars. No higher. And you tell me *exactly* what answers I have to learn. No more of these practice questions."

"This book," I began, holding up the source of the practice questions, "is an exact reproduction of the FAA exam." I pronounced each word slowly so there would be no ambiguity. "It has eight hundred questions. When you take the exam you will only have to answer fifty of these questions. There is no way of knowing in advance *which* fifty will be on your individual test."

Ahmed leaned across the table. I smelled sweat, the nauseatingly strong Polo cologne all the foreign students seemed to wear (another status symbol, I was sure), and stale cigarette smoke.

"You can find out, though," he said, no longer smiling. It wasn't like Ahmed to be so serious, and I wondered if the idea of being sent home in disgrace was finally sinking in. "I would be very *grateful*."

"I can't find out," I said lightly. "I'm not the examiner, remember?"

"I need to pass the test," Ahmed continued, staring at my breasts. The door was closed, and the cubbyhole of an office the academy had assigned to me was all the way at the end of a long, empty hall. I was starting to get nervous.

"You can't buy everything you want," I said in my best professional voice. "There are some things you have to *work* for."

"Three thousand is my final offer," he said, running his tongue across his lips.

"I'm going to get a drink of water," I said, hoping I didn't sound as scared as I felt. "I'm going to try to forget we had this conversation. When I get back, we're going to go over the questions you missed."

"Four thousand," Ahmed said, grabbing hold of my left hand. "It's very important to me."

"Let go," I said, trying to pull away. Ahmed had a surprisingly strong grip.

"I want to stay in America," he whispered, stroking my palm with his thumb. "This is the only way."

I grabbed my backpack with my right hand and swung it at Ahmed's head.

"Are you crazy?" he howled, letting go of my hand to clutch at his face. "I could get a bloody nose!"

I bolted for the door, opened it, and ran into the hall, where I stood taking deep breaths. Two flight instructors walked by having an animated conversation about airline pay scales. The janitor came out of an empty classroom wheeling his cart of cleaning supplies. The sound of laughter radiated from the lobby where students were watching TV between classes and flights. An engine was started out on the ramp. And Kalil, who I recognized as Ahmed's friend, was leaning against the wall opposite my office, smoking.

"Everything okay?" he asked.

"No," I said, walking to the water fountain.

"Ahmed, he gives you trouble?"

I didn't respond, but Kalil apparently knew Ahmed well.

"I'll talk to him," he said, crushing the butt of his cigarette beneath one of his Gucci loafers. "Stay here." Kalil went into my office and shut the door.

I turned on the water and took a long drink. At any other flight school the students I tutored would have been expelled long ago. But the academy only expelled students who ran out of money. Which was the reason, the director of ground training had explained, I had a job.

"Everything is taken care of," Kalil said, coming out of my

office. "Ahmed *will* do what you tell him. He *will* pass his test. I will stay here in case you need me."

I peered in the door. Ahmed was studying the book of questions, moving his lips as he read. I entered the room, propping open the door with my backpack. Ahmed looked up.

"We're wasting time!" he yelled. "I need to know the answers to these dumb questions!"

It was sometime after Ahmed failed the private pilot written exam for the fifth time and was summoned home by his disgusted family that I began to notice Kalil everywhere I went.

"That boy is infatuated with you," Anna, my flight instructor, said as I preflighted the Duchess, the four-seat twin-engine airplane the academy used for multiengine training.

"He's lonely because his friend flunked out," I said, draining fuel from the right wing.

"He looks lovesick to me," Anna said, tossing the beach bag that served as her combined purse and flight case into the backseat. I'd thought my mother would be pleased to know I had a woman flight instructor, especially a woman as experienced as Anna (she had over ten thousand hours of flight time, had flown five different types of business jets, and was the academy's FAA-designated examiner), but since my mother assumed that any intelligent woman who made a career of flying was mentally unbalanced, telling her about Anna had backfired.

"Don't scare me," I said, looking toward the building. Sure enough, Kalil was standing in the doorway staring at me.

"That's how it starts," Anna said, bending down to tie her sneaker. Her long, flowered skirt dragged on the ground. "First they watch you from a distance. Then they follow you. Then they give you gifts. Then they start paying your rent. The next thing you know—"

"This is not going to get beyond the following stage," I assured her.

"Just remember what happened to Janine," she warned. Janine had been Anna's (and the academy's) last woman student, over two years ago. "All that potential wasted just because she wanted a diamond ring. *He* promised she'd be able to fly the family's 747, and she believed him. Now she's somewhere in Dubai locked up in a harem!"

"I know," I said. I'd heard this story many times.

"I don't want that to happen to you, Kendra. The industry can't afford to lose qualified women pilots."

"Don't worry," I said, finishing my preflight and climbing into the left seat. Anna got into the right, pulling her skirt in behind her so it wouldn't get caught in the door (twice we'd had to land to reclose her door after it came open in flight).

"What are we going to work on today?" I asked, starting the left engine. Anna didn't follow a set syllabus. We jumped from commercial maneuvers to instrument procedures to multiengine training randomly. She believed in showing me each new maneuver once, having me practice it a few times, and then moving on.

"I think we'll do single engine approaches," she said, adjusting her sunglasses on her head. I had never seen Anna wear her sunglasses over her eyes; she used them only to keep her frizzy, graying hair out of her face.

It had been over a week since my last multiengine lesson, but that didn't stop Anna from retarding one of the mixture control levers to cutoff to simulate an engine failure immediately after takeoff.

"Some warm-up time would be nice," I protested.

"The procedure for a failed engine," Anna said, clearly enjoying herself as I struggled to get the airplane under control, "is supposed to be ingrained in your memory."

"Mixture, prop, throttle," I recited, fumbling with the six levers. "Identify, verify, feather."

"Which engine is it?"

"Dead foot, dead engine," I said, noting that my right foot was flat on the floor and my left foot was exerting considerable pressure on the left rudder pedal. "So it's the right." I retarded the right throttle to confirm my suspicions and then reached for the lever to feather it. Anna stopped me, though, because it was dangerous to feather an engine at low altitude unless it had *really* failed.

"Fly the pattern," she said.

At the end of two hours in the air, we'd practiced engine failures on the runway, after takeoff, turning crosswind, on downwind, base, and final approach. I was exhausted.

"You might as well take your multiengine checkride this week," Anna said as we taxied in.

"I only have eight hours," I said. The average number of hours to get a multiengine rating is ten.

"We've done all the maneuvers," she said. "There's no point in waiting until you forget them."

"Shouldn't we have a review?" I asked.

"Why waste the money? You still have all the other ratings to finish up."

The day after I passed my multiengine checkride, a dozen roses arrived in my office. The card said only "Congratulations," but I knew they were from Kalil. He'd passed into the gift-giving stage.

"Nice flowers," Rafi, a new meal ticket, commented. He was small and thin and looked no more than twelve, but I knew from his file that he was nineteen. At least fifty gold chains hung around his neck. "You have special boyfriend?"

"No," I answered. Although Karen had introduced me to some of her unattached medical school classmates, between my schedule of flying, studying, tutoring, working on my résumé, and waitressing (not to mention *their* schedules), there hadn't been a lot of time left over to pursue relationships.

"You want boyfriend?" he asked, cracking his gum. I didn't allow anyone to smoke in my office, so most of my tutees (all of whom were chain-smokers) wound up chewing gum throughout their sessions.

"No," I said firmly, flipping through Rafi's tests. He'd scored in the nineties on the first three, but on the fourth he'd gotten only a sixty.

"I would like American girlfriend," Rafi said.

"I don't understand this," I said, laying out the four tests. "You did well on these three, but you failed the final exam, which had a lot of the same questions."

"That's because Mohammed didn't come to class," he said.

"What does Mohammed have to do with it?" I had a feeling I didn't want to know.

"I sit next to Mohammed," Rafi said matter-of-factly. "He always knows right answers."

"That's cheating."

Rafi shrugged.

"Do you want to get your license?"

"Of course," he answered, chewing vigorously.

"Then you can't cheat anymore," I said, struggling for patience.

"Okay," he answered. "No problem."

As we went over the questions, Rafi demonstrated that he wasn't stupid. It was probably a sign of status to cheat.

Kalil had a way of finding out which airplane I was flying, and each day when I came out to preflight I found a different flower in the left seat.

"I don't think you should work here as a flight instructor," Anna said, putting that day's flower, a lily, behind her ear. Anna felt she was entitled to some of the flowers for being my instructor.

"Why not?" I asked, starting the engine. The academy was so pleased with my tutoring abilities, they'd offered me a full-time flight instructor position as soon as I got the rating.

"I don't want to see you ruin your career." She picked up the microphone and requested an instrument clearance to Stockton. It was too foggy for visual flying, but since I was working on my instrument rating anyway, Anna decided we'd practice the real thing.

"Who else would hire me with no experience?" I asked. "This would at least pay the rent."

"You'll have no trouble finding a job," Anna said. "Most flight schools want their flight instructors to be brand new. That way they don't have to pay you much." We taxied to the runway and were cleared for takeoff.

"You realize I've never flown in a cloud before, right?" I asked, nervous about Anna's tendency to forget I was a beginner.

"Just follow the clearance," Anna said. "It's the same as being under the hood." I'd had several lessons under the hood—an elongated white plastic visor meant to block my vision from the front and side windows, forcing me to fly strictly by reference to the instruments on the panel—but I'd known I could always peek out the windows simply by moving my head. This would be my first flight in actual instrument conditions.

We took off, and I concentrated on the instruments, trying to keep my scan moving and not allowing myself to become distracted by the clouds.

"The foreign men won't take you seriously as an instructor," Anna said, sticking round rubber disks over the heading and attitude indicators. "They're not used to taking criticism from women. They'll be running to a male instructor the minute you make a suggestion."

"They take you seriously," I mentioned.

"That's because I give the checkrides," she said. "And I've failed enough of them so they respect my authority."

"Cessna five-four-Juliett, turn right to a heading of zero-three-zero," the controller said.

Anna answered the radio, and I started the right turn. Since she'd covered up the heading indicator, my only directional information was coming from the magnetic compass—easy enough to read in straight and level flight but prone to disconcerting errors in turns. Errors such as indicating a turn in the opposite direction when turning from a northerly heading, as we were doing. At least Anna had left me the turn coordinator, an instrument depicting the airplane's wings, so I knew we were turning in the proper direction.

"Watch your altitude," Anna said. "We're on a real clearance. Three hundred feet off is a violation."

I must have pulled the nose up when I started the turn because we were climbing. I pushed the nose down to what I thought was level, but that wasn't easy either, since Anna had covered up the attitude indicator as well.

"I'm getting sick," Anna moaned in mock seriousness. "And if

I'm getting sick, imagine how your poor, scared passengers are going to feel."

I consulted the vertical speed indicator. We were descending at a thousand feet per minute. I pulled the nose up to correct.

"Heading," Anna warned.

I'd been so concerned about altitude, I'd forgotten to stop the turn. I cranked the control wheel to the left. The compass showed us passing zero-five-zero, a violation for sure. But that was just northerly turning error, I told myself. We were turning left. We couldn't be going further east.

"Five-four-Juliett, climb and maintain five thousand," the controller said.

Anna acknowledged and looked at me expectantly.

I added full power and raised the nose. Without the attitude indicator to show how much to pitch up, I had to use the vertical speed indicator, which lagged behind our actual position.

When I finally got us established on a five-hundred-foot-per-minute climb and steady on a heading of zero-three-zero, Anna decided to give me a brief respite and took the covers off the two instruments. It was suddenly much easier to control the airplane. I even had time to look out the windows and admire the clouds. Anna smiled, having known all along that by making it as hard as possible in the beginning it would seem much easier later. I would have to remember that for my own students.

"When I started flying, the airlines weren't hiring women pilots," Anna said, returning to our earlier conversation. "I had to take whatever jobs I could get. A few years ago, the academy was a good place to work. It was filled up with guys using their GI Bill benefits. They were motivated. They worked hard. Nothing like who we have now."

"You could go to another flight school," I suggested.

"This job is okay—for me," she said. "I get to pick and choose who I instruct. The hours are decent, and the pay is adequate."

"But with all your experience, you must be able to find a better job," I said.

"I'm too old, Kendra. Airlines and corporations don't hire pilots over forty. You're lucky you were born into a time when you'll have better opportunities."

When I passed my instrument checkride, I found two dozen roses in my office. A week later, when I passed my commercial checkride, I found Kalil in my office.

"Congratulations," he said, sitting down in the meal-ticket chair. He was holding a neatly wrapped package the size of a shoe box. "You are commercial-instrument pilot now."

"Are you here to sign up for tutoring?" I asked, pretending I didn't see the package. I opened a can of juice and drank deeply. It had been a difficult checkride, and I was drained.

"Of course not," Kalil said, putting a piece of gum into his mouth. "I pass all my exams. I have brought a special gift to you." He pushed the box across my desk.

"You've given me too many gifts already," I said, pushing it back.

"Please open it," he said. "It would mean so much to me."

Inside the box I found a Barbie-size doll dressed in a pink-and-gold belly dancer outfit. It was the most ridiculous thing I had ever seen. I had to hold my breath to keep from laughing.

"This is very . . . original, Kalil," I said, studying the doll's heavily made-up face and bright yellow hair. "Does it have some special significance?"

"The hair is just like yours. I thought you would like it."

"Thank you," I said, knowing Anna was going to have a few choice words to say about the doll. "It's very thoughtful." I was dying to go home and take a shower, but Kalil seemed to have no intention of leaving my office.

"So, you start work on your flight instructor rating now?" he asked.

"Tomorrow," I answered, wondering if Karen would be willing to take a study break and go out for Thai food. Even though I'd taken so many checkrides lately they were becoming routine, I still felt that a small celebration was in order.

"I work on my private pilot still," he said. "I plan to get commercial pilot, helicopter . . . if my father will allow it. I am fourth son. Fourth son is always pilot. Oldest brother, he takes over family business. He went to Harvard. You know Harvard?"

I nodded, fumbling around in my backpack for my car keys and hoping Kalil would get the hint.

"Next brother, he is doctor. He learned in Canada. Brother after that, he is lawyer. He studied in England."

"You have a very accomplished family," I said, tossing my keys from hand to hand.

"My father has many airplanes, you know. Gulfstreams, Citations, a Boeing. But I like helicopters best."

"I hope you get to fly them," I said, standing up and making my way to the door. "And thanks for the flowers and the doll."

Kalil finally stood up. "I have very much enjoyed talking with you," he said.

"It's been interesting," I agreed. "I'm sure I'll see you around."

"You're not going to believe what he gave me," I told Anna the next day. We were doing touch-and-go's and I was finding it very difficult to make a decent landing from the right seat, where I was sitting as part of my flight instructor training.

"The centerline is there for a reason," Anna said, as we touched down way to the left.

"A belly dancer doll," I said, steering back toward the center of the runway. "With yellow hair."

"Janine's belly dancer doll had red hair," she said gravely. "Just like hers."

"I don't think he meant anything by it," I said, pushing the power up for takeoff.

"We'll see," Anna said. "Climb up to fifty-five hundred. We'll do some spins."

"Spins?" Stalls were bad enough, but spins were much, much worse. I felt myself starting to sweat.

"Spin entries and recoveries are required for the flight instructor rating. Three in each direction."

Somewhere in the back of my mind I must have known that I would have to do spins in order to become a flight instructor, but I hadn't been expecting them on my first lesson in the right seat.

"I don't think I'm prepared today," I said.

"There's no preparation necessary," Anna said. "I'll talk you through them."

"I think I have a problem with spins," I continued weakly.

"What kind of problem?" Anna asked.

"I don't like them."

"Have you ever done one?"

"Not really."

"Then how do you know you don't like them?"

"I just know," I said, leveling off. "I can't do them, Anna. I really can't."

"I'll do the first one," Anna said. "Watch carefully." And before I could protest further, Anna had cut the power, pulled the airplane up into a stall, and kicked in full left rudder. The nose dropped straight down, and the airplane started to spin.

I screamed.

"I'm surprised at you, Kendra," Anna said, bringing us back to straight and level. "You've been one of my best students up until now. You got through your commercial, instrument, and multiengine ratings so quickly I was sure you were going to breeze right through your flight instructor. But now you pull this screaming act. I don't understand it."

"I just have . . . this thing about spins," I said meekly. Anna had been flying so long she wasn't afraid of anything.

"I have *this thing* about crashing," Anna said. "That's why I know how to recover from spins. Your students will get you into all kinds of crazy situations. As an instructor you have to know how to keep them from killing themselves. And, more importantly, from killing you. Are you sure you want to be an instructor?"

"You know I want to be an instructor," I said.

"Good," she said. "Tell you what, we'll count my first spin as one of your entries. Okay?"

"Anna," I whimpered from the right seat, "I just don't think I can do this."

"What are you afraid of, Kendra?" she asked gently.

"Losing control," I whispered. My mother was right. Flying was crazy. I was crazy. Maybe I did need professional help.

"That's why we're doing this," she said, turning to face me. "So you'll always be in control. It's very important to be in control, especially for a woman in this field. Let me tell you a story.

"My first jet job was with a corporation down in LA, close to ten years ago. I'd never flown a jet, and I'd never flown in the LA area. But I had about six thousand hours, a lot of them multiengine, and the president of the company liked the idea of a woman pilot. So, the chief pilot took me up to check me out in their Learjet. At first he was very professional, showing me how things worked and pointing out landmarks. But as soon as we climbed above ten thousand feet, he clicked on the autopilot, took off his seat belt, and grabbed me."

"What did you do?" I asked, mortified.

"He told me that if I said no I'd never have a job in this industry again. He said he'd tell everyone I was too emotional to fly a jet. He said it would be my word against his."

"Wasn't there anyone you could tell?"

"Who would have believed me?" Anna asked. "Plus, husband number two had just walked out with no forwarding address, and I was alone with two kids to support. I *needed* that job."

I didn't know what to say.

"You see, Kendra, I felt like I had no control. Like there was nothing I could do to stop what was happening. It was a terrible feeling. I hope you never experience being out of control like that. You need to be tough to survive in this industry, Kendra. Do you think you're tough enough?"

"Okay," I said, feeling ashamed of my pathetic fear in the face of what Anna had been through. "I'll try to do the spins."

"Good girl," Anna said. "I'd hate to see you give up now."

The day after passing my flight instructor checkride, I came back to the academy to pack up my office. I'd been hired by a flight school across the bay, and I was starting tomorrow. I'd been in my office no more than five minutes when Kalil knocked on the door.

"You are leaving," he said, making himself comfortable in the meal-ticket chair.

"I have a job flight instructing," I said, stuffing books into cartons I'd picked up at a liquor store.

"Have you ever considered marriage?" Kalil asked.

"I'm only twenty-three," I said, taping together a carton. I had five full shelves of flying books (which Karen was not going to be happy to see infiltrating our apartment), and I wondered how they were all going to fit into the car.

"I think you should consider marriage with me," Kalil said.

I dropped the stack of books I'd been holding.

"I hardly know you, Kalil," I stammered, trying to retrieve the fallen books.

"Marriage is an arrangement," he said. "You will know me in time."

"But I don't want to get married," I said. "I'm just beginning my career."

"I'll pay your parents thirty thousand dollars cash," Kalil continued. "Maybe a little more because you are blond."

I listened in horrified fascination.

"You will have your own suite of rooms and your own servants. You will have an unlimited clothing and jewelry allowance and be permitted to visit your parents once a year."

"I don't really think I'm the right woman for you," I interrupted, wanting to hear more yet feeling obligated to stop Kalil before he got too carried away.

"Don't answer now," he said, standing up to leave. "Americans like to think about things. Think about my offer."

"There's nothing to think about," I said, forcing myself to look up at Kalil. "I absolutely cannot marry you, Kalil. It's just out of the question. I'm sure you'll be able to find someone more suitable—"

"But you are the woman I want," he pleaded. "Would your parents consider forty thousand? I'm sure my father would approve that amount."

"I'm not for sale," I said, taping together the last box of books and surveying the shelves. The only thing left was the belly dancer doll.

"Everyone is for sale," he said. "For the right price."

"I think you should take this back," I said, handing him the doll.

"That was made especially for you," Kalil said coldly. "You will keep it."

"Fine," I said, setting the doll on the empty desk and having a flash of what must have happened to Janine. How she'd been flattered and excited by the initial attention and romance, the expensive gifts, the meals at elegant restaurants. How she'd been impressed by his wealth and intrigued by the idea of becoming a princess in an exotic country. How, as a newly licensed pilot, she'd been tantalized by the idea of flying a jumbo jet. And then how she'd gotten to the palace, allowed him to put her passport "somewhere safe," and been told in no uncertain terms how she was expected to behave. I got chills just thinking about it. I couldn't wait to get out of this place and away from these men. I lifted a box and began carrying it to the car.

"You will change your mind," he said, following me empty-handed.

"I don't think so," I said, loading the box into the trunk and going back for the next.

"I have my flying lesson now," he called as I walked past him with the second box. "I'll expect to hear from you soon."

I finished loading the boxes and returned to my office for my backpack. The doll was still where I'd left it on the desk. I took one last look at it and left it for the next tutor to discover and wonder about.

CLIMBS AND DESCENTS

U nlike most of the flight instructors at Bart's Aviation Services, I enjoyed teaching. I liked my students and the challenges they presented. I found it satisfying and rewarding to watch them progress from timid and terrified beginners to safe and confident pilots. It was good for my ego to be trusted, respected, and admired. And there were things about flight instructing that even my mother found acceptable. She could now tell people I was teaching full-time (she didn't tell them *what* I was teaching, of course), and, for some reason, she didn't seem to think flight instructing was as dangerous as "flying," because she'd never come across an article in *The New York Times* (from which she clipped every article related to the inherent dangers of aviation) about an *instructor* being involved in a plane crash.

But I missed being a pilot. Even though I did occasionally get to demonstrate maneuvers to my students, it wasn't the same as flying a trip by myself. And it wasn't anywhere close to wearing a light blue, epaulet shirt with four stripes on each shoulder and flying passengers in a six- or eight-seat twin to exciting destinations, the way charter pilots did.

Although Bart's paid less than the other flight schools in the Bay Area, and although it was at Concord Airport—an hour's drive from the apartment I shared with Karen in San Francisco—Bart's had a charter department into which flight instructors were promised advancement after a year of teaching. I'd been at Bart's fourteen months and eleven days, making me (except for the chief flight instructor) the most senior flight instructor Bart had. As soon as I finished my lesson with Scott, I was going to have a meeting with Bart to discuss my transition into the charter department.

But first Scott had to make two good touch-and-go's in a row so I could let him solo. He didn't know that, of course. It was my prerogative as the instructor to keep it a secret until the last minute, when I would vacate the right seat, leaving him alone in the left. The theory was that if the student knew he might solo, he'd waste the lesson worrying instead of learning.

"Aaaaaaaah," I wailed, as Scott slammed the airplane onto the runway. He raised the flaps, pushed the throttle forward, and began the takeoff roll.

"What's the matter?" he asked. "I landed on the centerline and within the first third of the runway." Those were two of my criteria for acceptable landings.

"That was not a *landing*," I said. "That was an *arrival*."

"Did I hurt you, baby?" he asked the instrument panel, stroking it lovingly. "I tried to be gentle, but sometimes I get carried away—"

"A good pattern is the key to a good landing," I said, ignoring Scott's romantic interlude with the airplane. He was twenty, in love with flying and windsurfing. "What was wrong with the last pattern?"

"Nothing," he answered, smiling. "It was flawless."

"It was not *flawless*," I said. "You were too close in on downwind, which made you high on base. When you saw that you were high, you pushed the nose down without reducing power. Consequently you were too fast on final, which is why you hit so hard." Scott was actually one of my better students. Flying came naturally to him, and his biggest problem was overconfidence. Periodically I felt compelled to remind him he was still a beginner, even if it meant exaggerating his faults.

"Well, this is going to be a good one," he assured me.

And, in fact, his next two landings were greasers.

"I can't take much more of this abuse," I said. "Taxi over to the tower and let me out."

"You're getting out?" Scott asked, paling beneath his windsurfer's tan.

"Do three full-stop landings," I said, certifying in his logbook that I found him competent to solo. "And don't hesitate to go around if you don't like the way an approach looks, okay?" Scott's cockiness did not lend itself well to go-arounds.

"Okay," Scott said, recovering his poise. "Now leave me alone with my baby."

I climbed out of the airplane and raced up the six flights of stairs to the tower.

"Hi, Kendra," Kyle called as I reached the top of the stairs. Kyle, the controller working ground control, was one of my favorites. He was a pilot himself and had also been a flight instructor until his wife became pregnant with triplets and he was forced to find a more secure job. "How are things at Bart's?"

"Too many instructors, not enough students," I said, sitting down on a stool to catch my breath.

"I hear Bart is buying two new Navajos just for charter," Kyle said. Piper Navajos are ten-seat, twin-engine airplanes.

"They're supposed to be coming next week," I said, watching Scott taxi toward the runway.

"When are you getting checked out?" Kyle asked.

"I'm going to talk to Bart this afternoon. I don't think he realizes I've been here over a year."

"Cherokee one-zero-Papa is ready for takeoff," Scott's voice announced over the loudspeaker. "Requesting closed traffic."

"Runway one left," Nancy, the controller working airborne traffic, told Scott. "Make left closed traffic. Cleared for takeoff."

"Bet you'll be glad to get out of flight instructing," Kyle said.

"I don't mind teaching," I said. "I was even thinking of hanging on to some of my students, working with them on my days off. But I need multiengine time if I'm ever going to get an airline job." I walked from window to window, watching Scott. He was on downwind, flying parallel to the runway, just where he was supposed to be. Scott was my eleventh student to solo, but that didn't make it any easier. A flight instructor could never be exactly sure how a student would cope with being alone in an airplane.

"Nice day for a first solo," Kyle mused. "No wind. No traffic. I wish I was up there flying instead of being trapped in this glass cage."

"How are the kids?" I asked.

"Toddling all over the place and into everything."

Scott's first landing was good, I noted with relief. But as he began his second pattern, traffic started to pick up. When Scott called in on downwind, Nancy told him he was number three, behind a Cessna.

Being number three was routine at our busy airport, and Scott had plenty of experience following other airplanes around the pattern. From my vantage point in the tower I could see the Cessna ahead and to his right. He should have responded to Nancy by either calling the Cessna "in sight" or saying he was "looking." But he continued flying a normal pattern, getting closer and closer to the Cessna.

"What's with your student up there?" Nancy asked.

"Maybe you should tell him to widen out," I suggested.

"I can control my own traffic, thank you," she said. "I was just wondering if he had a hearing problem."

Kyle gave me a sympathetic look.

"One-zero-Papa, your traffic is at one o'clock, less than half a mile! Do you have it in sight?" Nancy's voice had taken on a shrill, panicky quality. Scott was heading straight for the Cessna.

My heart began to beat faster.

"One-zero-Papa, make an IMMEDIATE left three-sixty!" Nancy shouted into her microphone. "NOW, one-zero-Papa!"

"Traffic in sight," Scott finally announced, making S-turns to stay behind the Cessna instead of the left three-sixty Nancy had ordered.

"Your judgment is a little questionable here," she grumbled in my direction.

"First solos are unpredictable," I said. "They sometimes get nervous and temporarily forget everything they've ever learned."

As if illustrating my point, Scott's second landing was a disaster. He bounced three times before he got the airplane on the ground.

"You want me to have him park it?" Kyle asked, before issuing Scott taxi instructions.

"Give him one more chance," I said.

Scott taxied back to the runway and took off. His third pattern was textbook perfect. I was about to thank the controllers and start down the stairs when I saw him go around.

Nancy cleared him to fly the pattern again, and I sat back down to watch. At the end of another perfect pattern, Scott went around again.

"What's his problem now?" Nancy asked.

"He must have been uncomfortable with his approach," I said, starting to sense that maybe Scott was playing games.

"Well, he's screwing up my traffic pattern," Nancy muttered.

On his third try Scott landed, and I went to meet him on the ramp. Normally, I didn't critique students' first solos. It was enough that they survived. But I couldn't let Scott get off so easily.

"Was there a reason for the go-arounds?" I asked in my firmest instructor voice.

"I was having too much fun to stop so soon," he said, loading on the charm. "You did say only three *landings*."

I sighed. "If I can't trust you up there, I can't let you solo again."

"Don't be mad, Kendra," Scott said, lifting me up in a bear hug and carrying me toward the flight school. "I'm fine. The airplane's fine. It's a beautiful day. And I soloed!"

"Put me down." I laughed, pounding on Scott's back.

"I soloed!" Scott announced, carrying me through Bart's. "I defied the laws of gravity and lived to tell about it!"

A few flight instructors stuck their heads out of the office and congratulated Scott. The secretary and the receptionist, neither of whom had ever attempted to conceal their admiration of Scott's physical attributes, also congratulated him.

"Put me down, Scott," I insisted as Bart, the owner and president of Bart's Aviation Services, descended the stairs from his office.

"Hey, Bart! I soloed," Scott declared, whirling me around.

"Congratulations," Bart said. "Make sure Kendra puts your name on the board." The huge, airplane-shaped blackboard was in the lobby as you entered Bart's. It listed the names of all customers who had recently soloed or acquired new ratings. Sometimes names stayed up there for years because Bart wanted people who came in to think he had the most successful flight school in the state.

"I'll do it right now," I said.

Scott finally put me down, wanting his name on the board more than he wanted to keep me in the air. He watched as I wrote out his full name and the day's date under FIRST SOLOS. Then, satisfied to see his accomplishment duly recorded, he kissed the hands of both the secretary and receptionist, gave me a final hug, and raced out the front door to celebrate with an afternoon of windsurfing.

Since I had half an hour to kill before my meeting with Bart, I retreated to the instructors' office to have lunch. The office was a cramped, windowless room where Bart's fourteen flight instructors shared four desks, eight chairs, and two file cabinets. The office was empty except for Tom, the chief flight instructor, who was working on his résumé. I pulled out a chair and unwrapped my sandwich.

"Did you hear the news?" Tom asked.

"No," I said, between bites.

"Bart hired three new instructors."

"Any women?" I asked. I was currently the only woman flight instructor at Bart's, and I couldn't help hoping he would hire another. I was on friendly enough terms with all the guys, but it would be nice to have another woman around—someone I could talk to about more than just flying.

"One," Tom said. "The problem is, we don't have enough business to support fourteen flight instructors, let alone seventeen!"

"What's her name?" I asked.

"Tracy something," he said, working himself into a rage. "And do you know what that tyrant Bart said?"

"What?"

"He said hiring those three would be good for business because it would force us to look harder for students. Can you believe that crap!" Tom picked up his logbook and threw it across the room. "I've had it with this place! I've been here for two years, and I still don't have enough students to fill up the day. Last month I had to borrow money from my girlfriend to pay the rent!" Tom had turned down a position in the charter department in favor of becoming chief flight instructor because Bart had promised it would yield more money. What Bart had meant, Tom later learned, was that he would have the *potential* to increase his earnings by giving checkrides. But he would still be responsible for bringing in his own business and would still be paid only by actual hours flown.

"Why don't you tell Bart you've changed your mind and you want to go into the charter department?" I picked up Tom's logbook and carried it over to his desk. It was the same logbook I used, *The Standard Pilot Master Log*, but whereas mine was barely a quarter filled and still looked shiny and new, his was battered and stained and almost full. I wondered if I would ever have that many hours.

"I already told him," Tom said, shaking his head. "He said charter pilots are a dime a dozen, but good chief flight instructors are hard to find."

"How's the résumé?"

"I'm sending it to every commuter on the West Coast," he said. "I don't want to move, but I'm at the point where I'll go anywhere to get out of this place—"

"We've got company," I whispered, nodding toward the door where Bart was standing with two men and a woman.

"There you are, Tom," Bart said. He had his arm around the woman, and the men were standing behind him. Clearly these were the new flight instructors. "Since I'm booked all afternoon, I assumed you wouldn't mind showing the new guys and gal around."

"Not at all," Tom said through clenched teeth.

"I'll see you kids tomorrow morning at eight sharp," Bart said, patting the woman on the back and pushing her toward Tom. Tom shook hands with her and then the two men.

"As you can see," he began while I finished my peanut-butter sandwich and juice, "we're a little short on space. With four desks and *now* seventeen instructors—well, you can do the math . . ."

I waved to Tom and headed upstairs.

Bart's office was on the second floor of the building, overlooking the ramp and runways. The paneled walls were covered with memorabilia from Bart's twenty years as a navy pilot.

When I entered, Bart was at his desk studying a framed photograph.

"Did I ever tell you about the time I got shot down over North Vietnam?" Bart asked, motioning me to a chair.

"When you ate the snake?" Bart used our staff meetings as occasions to tell war stories, and I'd heard them all before.

"There I was, in the middle of the jungle, bruised and bloodied, without food or water, wondering how much longer I could survive, when this snake slithered across my legs . . ."

I waited patiently for Bart to finish his story.

"So, to what do I owe the pleasure of your company?" he finally asked.

"I've been here over a year now," I began, thinking he would understand the significance of "over a year."

"I guess you have," Bart said. "You were hired in April, right? Just out of flight school, I believe?"

"That's right," I said. "I've enjoyed flight instructing, but—"

"And you've gained a lot of good experience here," he interrupted. "I've watched you develop into a confident and knowledgeable instructor. I've seen you with the students, and they seem to like you. You do your job well, Kendra. I'm very pleased."

"Thank you," I said. "But now that I've been here *over a year,* I'm ready to advance into the charter department."

"But if you enjoy flight instructing, why would you want to fly charter?" Bart appeared confused.

"I miss *flying,*" I said. "Teaching people how to land isn't the same as making the landings myself."

"I see your point," he said reasonably. "But I've never thought of you as having charter potential, Kendra."

"Charter potential?"

"I'm constantly evaluating our flight instructors for charter potential, from the moment they walk through the door. Those new kids I hired today, they all have it. They're not going to have to teach for long before *they* move up. But when I first saw you, Kendra, I said to myself, now there's a dedicated flight instructor. She's going to do real well for me." Bart smiled at me. "And you certainly have. My first impressions are never wrong."

"I don't understand," I said. *Everyone* who stuck out the first year at Bart's moved up into the charter department. Some instructors even bought their blue shirts the day they were hired so they would be ready when their year was up. "I've been here *over a year,* I have all my instructor ratings, I have almost a thousand hours, and everyone compliments my landings."

"Those are all admirable accomplishments," Bart said. "But let's be realistic. In the most important ways, you're just not charter pilot material."

"What important ways?"

"Looks, for one thing," Bart said. "You don't *look* like a charter pilot. Charter pilots don't have long hair."

"I'll get my hair cut," I suggested. Though my hair hung halfway down my back, and I always wore it in a ponytail or braid to work, maybe it was time for a more grown-up look. "How short should it be?"

"Now, don't go cutting that pretty hair," Bart said. "That's not the only problem anyway. It's also those books you read. Charter pilots don't sit around reading. They spend time in the hangar. They talk to the mechanics. They get their hands dirty."

"I only read when a student cancels," I said defensively. Bart required his flight instructors to be at the flight school at least eight hours a day, rain or shine, whether lessons were scheduled or not. Yet he only paid us a percentage of the time we billed our students. It was therefore possible to come to the airport, have four or five students cancel, and not make a penny—or have anything to do— for the day. Which is why I still waitressed three nights a week and always carried a book around.

"But you read where customers can *see* you. Being a charter pilot is an attitude. It's a certain . . . professionalism. When customers charter an airplane, they expect the pilot to look like . . . well, like a pilot." Bart smiled, satisfied with his explanation.

"You mean, like a man?" I asked, unable to hide my sarcasm. I couldn't help it. It was so unfair! I'd put in a over a year of long hours and little pay, all so I could fly charter, and now I couldn't because I didn't *look* the part.

"Not necessarily," Bart said, not seeming to notice my tone. "Our customers watch TV. They know there are lady pilots these days. They wouldn't balk at seeing one who looks like Tracy, for example." Tracy, I recalled, had been wearing unwrinklable polyester pants, a blouse buttoned up to her neck, a bow tie, and heels. She'd also had short hair. In contrast, I was wearing a pink cotton sundress and flat sandals. We were in the middle of a heat wave, and it was over a hundred degrees on the ramp, probably a hundred and ten in the airplanes. I thought I was dressed both sensibly and professionally. I couldn't help it if the dress was slightly rumpled from the heat.

"Look, Kendra," Bart said. "The bottom line is that our charter department is a *service* organization. We give the customers what they want, and they want pilots who look like pilots. Stick with what you're good at—flight instructing. Is money a problem? I'll give you a raise. Hell, you've been here over a year. How does eight dollars an hour sound?"

Eight dollars an hour was a dollar an hour more than I was making and meant that in a good month I might be able to take home as much as eight hundred dollars. An improvement, but still barely enough to pay my bills. If it hadn't been for my mother's periodic checks (with which she'd hoped I'd buy a new winter coat, a subscription to *The New Yorker*, or an Amtrak ticket back to New Jersey), I wouldn't have had any money for groceries.

"That's per billed hour, of course," Bart continued. "And you're still going to have to work hard to bill those hours. There's no such thing as a free lunch in this industry." He smiled and stood up. "Do we have a deal?"

"I don't know," I said, rising slowly, suddenly drained of energy. "I'd planned to stay here for a few more years. But now that there's no incentive . . ." I shrugged.

"You think things through," Bart said, staring at me as if he'd never seen me before. "You look nice in that dress, Kendra. Pink is a good color for you."

"Well, thanks for your time," I said, turning to leave.

"Hey," Bart said, grabbing me from behind and pulling me into a tight embrace, "how about a hug for old Bart? No hard feelings, okay?"

I left Bart's office in despair. In order to fly charter, I was going to have to change jobs and start at the bottom of another company. I'd wasted a whole year accruing useless seniority. And on top of all that, Bart had decided to hug me! I'd wanted to kick him in the balls and run from the room, but if I was going to get another job, I needed a good reference. This was the only flying job I'd had. So I'd stood stiffly while his disgusting paws fondled my ponytail, and tried not to fall over backward attempting to evade his pressing pelvis.

"Bobbie's out preflighting," the receptionist told me as I entered the lobby.

"What time did she start?" Bobbie was a very thorough preflighter. I usually scheduled her half an hour before I'd be ready so she'd have enough time to inspect every rivet on the airplane.

"About fifteen minutes ago," the receptionist said.

I found Bobbie lying on the ground under the airplane. Her long, tan legs were sticking out of her cutoff shorts, and her Grateful Dead T-shirt was splattered with grease.

"Kiddo," she called to me. "Check this out. I think I found some *corrosion.*"

I crawled under the airplane to look, wishing Bart were there to see. Maybe he'd revise his opinion of my charter potential. The corrosion turned out to be dirt I removed with my finger.

"How's the rest of the airplane?" I asked warily as we crawled out from underneath.

"It's fine," Bobbie said, standing up. "I had to tighten a few bolts, but that was no big deal." She handed me a large Safeway bag. "I brought you a surprise." Bobbie's surprises usually fell off the trucks her boyfriend drove. Today's surprise was several two-quart Tupperware canisters without their tops.

"Jimmy forgot the lids," Bobbie said. "But you can always use foil or plastic wrap."

"Thanks. Maybe I'll take one home, but not the whole bag." I had to keep reminding Bobbie that I lived in a very small apartment with a roommate who didn't like clutter.

"What are we going to work on today?" she asked, entering the airplane. "I read the section on minimum controllable airspeed, like you said."

"Good." I got in beside her. "We'll start with that and see how far we get." Bobbie tried hard, but she had trouble remembering from one lesson to the next. She could perform procedures that called for use of a checklist, but she was hopeless with commonsense and memory items.

Bobbie started the airplane and turned on the radio.

"How ya doing today, Kyle?" she said into the microphone, her way of requesting a taxi clearance. I didn't condone nonstandard phraseology on the radio, but Bobbie was careful to use it only for the male controllers who were known to appreciate her gruff, sexy voice.

"Happy as a clam," Kyle said. "Taxi to runway three-two right."

"Thanks, kiddo," Bobbie said, taxiing out.

"Brakes," I mentioned. Since checking the brakes was not written on the after-start checklist, I had to remind Bobbie to do it.

"Feel good to me," she said, stomping on them with such force I had to grab onto the instrument panel.

We eventually made it to the runway, and Nancy cleared us for takeoff. Bobbie released the brakes and pushed the throttle forward. We rolled down the runway, drifting farther and farther to the left.

"Right rudder," I suggested when contact with the grass seemed imminent.

"Damn! I always forget that pesky right rudder," Bobbie said. "What speed do we take off at again?"

"Sixty." We were at seventy-five and still on the runway.

She raised the nose, and the airplane jumped into the air.

"Climb to thirty-five hundred," I said, relaxing now that we were off the ground.

"So, how've you been, kiddo?" Bobbie always asked how I was when she wanted to tell me how *she* was. "You know that land Jimmy bought in Idaho with my flying money?" During Bobbie's last lesson I'd learned that Jimmy, her boyfriend, had used her flying money to buy a few acres in Idaho. Since Bobbie didn't have a job, and since she paid for her lessons in five-dollar bills, I had often wondered where this mysterious "flying money" came from. "Well, this week he came home with a trailer and said he's moving up there with or without me."

"Head out toward the valley," I said. "About thirty degrees to the right."

"It's technically my land, but I don't want to move because of my flying lessons."

"Thirty-five hundred," I reminded Bobbie as she climbed past our altitude.

She attempted to level off, but wound up three hundred feet too high.

"You can always continue your flying lessons out there," I said.

"Kiddo, I could *never* fly with another instructor," she said, trying to trim the airplane so it would maintain altitude.

"Thirty-*five* hundred," I said again.

"Why can't we just stay here?" Bobbie asked. "I've got it trimmed perfectly. See, no hands!" She took her hands off the controls to demonstrate that the airplane would stay where it was, at thirty-eight hundred feet.

"This is an illegal altitude," I said. "Also, it's sloppy flying."

"Okay, I'll go down." She began a shallow descent. "The reason I fly with you is because you're so patient. I know I'm not the greatest pilot, and I really appreciate how nice you are to me. Another instructor probably would have given up ages ago—"

"Clearing turns."

"Plus, I don't *want* to live in a trailer in Idaho," Bobbie added, making a left turn. "But Jimmy and I have been together eight years." Bobbie rolled into a right turn. "Do you think I should just throw away eight good years? I can't remember what to do next."

"Reduce power."

"Right." She reduced power. "It isn't easy to find a man like Jimmy. Now flaps?"

"Uh-huh."

"With this whole AIDS thing, you don't know who you can trust anymore. Now what?"

"Maintain altitude. Maintain heading. And slow it down until you hear the stall warning."

For the rest of the hour we worked on minimum controllable airspeed. Bobbie was doing it well at the end, but I knew she'd forget everything by the next lesson.

"You know, Bobbie," I began, as we were heading back to the airport, "I don't think you should base your Idaho decision on having me as an instructor."

"But you're the reason I stick with my flying lessons," she said.

"I might not be here forever."

"Did you get an airline job?" she asked, turning to look at me. The airplane went into a steep right bank. "Why didn't you tell me right away? We'll have a party!"

"Level the wings," I said. "And no, I need a lot of multiengine hours before an airline will hire me. But it doesn't look like I can get those hours at Bart's, so I'm going to have to go wherever I can find the best job."

"I thought you were going into the charter department. You said we'd still be able to fly together."

"That's what I thought, too. But Bart doesn't think I 'look' or 'act' like a charter pilot."

"What kind of bull doodie is that?"

"It's what he said."

"I'm going to give that slimy, military, chauvinist bastard a piece of my mind when we get back! He has no excuse to treat you like that!"

"Bobbie," I said, trying to calm her down. "I haven't quit yet. I don't want to get *fired*. Please don't say anything until I leave, okay?"

"If you leave," Bobbie said, "I'm leaving, too. And I'm telling Bart the Fart why."

"Fine," I said. "As long as you don't say anything until I'm gone."

Since I didn't have any other students after Bobbie, and since I felt sweaty and tired, desperate for a shower and a nap, I decided to go home early. If Bart didn't like it, too bad. When I was gone I hoped all my students would find other flight schools. I hoped Bart would lose every drop of business I'd brought in!

"Kendra, you're not leaving, are you?" Colby, one of my students, was coming in as I was going out.

"I was," I said. "What's up?" Colby was a lawyer, working on his private pilot's license. He'd almost finished his solo cross-countries, after which we'd start reviewing for his checkride.

"Do you think you could stay an extra hour and go up with me? I'd feel more comfortable doing the rest of my cross-countries if I had another lesson under the hood." Colby already had the usual hour of instrument practice I gave my students before they soloed, but he'd probably flown too near a cloud on one of his solo flights and scared himself. I could hardly say no to such a sensible request.

"If you really want me to—"

"You're a doll, Kendra. I'll pay you for *all* of your time—even when I'm preflighting." Since, after their first few lessons, students usually preflighted by themselves, I didn't start billing until I arrived at the airplane.

"You don't need to do that," I said.

"Don't question a billable hour. You want to eat, don't you?"

"I'll meet you out there in ten minutes," I said.

When Colby went out to preflight, I went to the instructors' office to get his training folder.

"Guess what?" Tom called from his desk. For a minute I thought he was reading a book and I'd have an ally against Bart, but then I saw it was an airplane manual.

"You got another job?"

"Sort of. Bart told me I can go full-time into the charter department. With the new Navajos and all the summer business, he needs pilots right away."

"Who's going to be chief flight instructor?" I asked, suddenly realizing that I wouldn't mind being chief flight instructor. And since Bart thought I was such a great flight instructor and had no charter potential anyway, it made perfect sense for him to promote me.

"Bart said he'd find somebody," Tom answered. "He wants to hire from outside the flight school. He says otherwise the instructors wouldn't respect the chief's authority. By the way, do you want my students? I only have a few serious ones, but you can call the others and try to get them back into the fold."

"Give your students to one of the new instructors," I said, overwhelmed with frustration. I was never going to get anywhere at Bart's. How could I have been so stupid not to have noticed sooner? "I'm quitting!" I grabbed the hood and Colby's folder and walked out of the office.

"What do you mean?" Tom called after me. "Things are just starting to get better around here."

I stormed out of the building onto the ramp. Colby had just finished his preflight and was settling into the left seat.

"Everything looks okay to me," he said.

"Good." I got in and slammed the door.

"I just want to work on the basics," he said, starting the engine. "Climbs, descents, and turns. Maybe some VOR tracking."

"Fine."

"I asked the firm if I could take a sabbatical for six months," he mentioned as we were climbing out. Colby was an associate at one of San Francisco's most prestigious law firms.

"Why would you take a sabbatical?" I asked out of politeness. I really wasn't in the mood to talk.

"I think I want to fly full-time."

"You'll have your license in less than a month," I said. "Then you can fly whenever you want."

"I'm seriously considering getting *all* my ratings," he said shyly.

"You can still get all your ratings without quitting your job," I said.

"But law is so boring. I want to do something interesting and exciting and challenging. Like flight instructing."

"Listen, Colby," I began. "Flight instructing is not the glamorous job you seem to think it is. You'll be extremely lucky if you can make a thousand dollars a month. You won't have your own desk or secretary or telephone. You'll have to hunt down your own students, and you'll have to show up even if they don't—"

"Don't you think I'm a good enough pilot?" he interrupted.

"Of course you're a good enough pilot. That's not the point."

"What *is* the point, then?"

"The point is that this job sucks!" I said, losing control. "There are no work rules or precedents or policy. They can do whatever they want because they don't care if you stay or quit! It costs them *nothing* to find and train new flight instructors! It's degrading, insulting, and offensive!"

"But you love your job, Kendra," Colby said, ignoring my outburst. "You're the one who inspired me to fly in the first place. You're always so excited and enthusiastic. Your love of flying is contagious."

I groaned inwardly. That wasn't the response I'd expected.

"Level off here and turn left to a heading of one-seven-zero," I said, reminding myself I was being paid to teach.

"If I go through my commercial, instrument, and instructor ratings at Bart's, will you be my instructor?" Colby asked.

"I don't think I'm going to be around here much longer," I answered. "The opportunities for advancement seem to be limited."

"I thought Bart has a charter department," Colby said, rolling out on the heading.

"He does," I said. "He just doesn't want me in it. Intercept the Stockton three-four-zero degree radial."

"Why not?" Colby asked, tuning his VOR receiver. "You'd be a great charter pilot."

"Bart thinks I'm not professional enough. He says I don't 'look' or 'act' like a charter pilot."

"That sounds like discrimination to me," Colby said. "Are all the charter pilots men?"

"Until today I was the only woman pilot, period, at Bart's. But he told me the woman he just hired will be moving into the charter department soon."

"I want to talk to one of the litigators in my office about this," Colby said. "You may be able to sue. Don't do anything until I get back to you."

"Even if I sued Bart and won, I couldn't work here anymore," I said, sighing. "Either way I'll have to just go someplace else and start over."

"That would be everyone's loss."

"I hope it's Bart's," I said. "I'll give some thought to who you should choose as your next instructor. And listen. If you really love to fly you should just go for it."

ALTITUDE

In the dream, I was flying a jet for a major airline. I was the captain, but the first officer was telling me what to do because my uniform hat (which had been designed for a man) kept slipping over my eyes and I couldn't see. We were flying low, over the ocean, and it was very dark. I was nervous because I didn't know how to land a jet, but the first officer said we wouldn't have to worry about landing if we just flew under the water. I didn't think the airplane was supposed to get wet, but I pushed the control wheel forward anyway. Just as the water started to splash over the windshield, the phone rang.

"Want a charter?" It was Dale, one of the pilots from Golden Gate Aviation, the Fixed Base Operation in Marin County, twenty miles north of San Francisco, where I was the senior charter pilot and, because there weren't many charters, also a flight instructor.

"I'm sleeping," I said as the dream faded. It was my first day off in two weeks. There had been a lot of business lately, and it was a well-known fact that charter pilots who weren't available on demand were quickly replaced by those with more enthusiasm.

"What about a *multiengine* charter?" Of course I wanted a multi-engine charter. I had almost 1,700 hours, but only 153.8 were in twins. Since commuter and major airlines wanted applicants to have at least a thousand multiengine hours, I usually jumped at any opportunity for multi time (especially because most of the charters at Golden Gate were in singles), but I hadn't gotten back from last night's (single-engine) charter until two in the morning, I had a terrible headache, and I was just too tired.

"No, thanks," I said.

"They want the Seneca . . ." That was really supposed to entice me. The Seneca was the company's newest airplane, a six-seat twin.

"Let Mark do it," I suggested. Out the window I could see that it was a foggy, drizzly day, and I wanted more than anything to take two aspirin and go back to sleep to finish my dream.

"He's taking his kids on an Easter egg hunt," Dale said. "You're the only one available." Dale didn't have enough hours to fly multiengine charters by himself, but he could act as copilot and still log the time.

"I'm just too tired," I said. "I wouldn't be safe."

Dale was strategically silent.

"Where is this charter going, anyway?" I finally asked, giving in as Dale knew I would. I just couldn't resist flying the Seneca.

"The guy wants to go to some private strip up north, then to Santa Monica, and then to Phoenix. It should be at least sixteen hours worth."

Sixteen hours! I was lucky if I got sixteen hours of multiengine time in three months. "What time?" I asked, pushing back the covers.

"Now," Dale said.

∞

When I got to the airport, Dale wasn't there and the receptionist was in tears. It seemed that the passengers wanted to pay by check, but they didn't have any identification. The receptionist didn't know what to do.

"Call Byron at home," I told her. Byron was the owner of the company.

The passengers, a couple dressed in identical black leather jumpsuits, were sitting on the couch across the lobby. As I approached, they stood up. The man looked to be in his mid-fifties. He was short, had a long gray ponytail, and was wearing mirrored glacier goggles with leather sides.

"Hi, babe," he said, holding out his hand. "I'm Dr. Brown, and this is my essential ingredient, Bo." Bo was taller than Dr. Brown and couldn't have been much over twenty-one. She was wearing huge, heart-shaped, purple sunglasses.

I introduced myself, shaking hands with both of them, and explained that in order for us to accept a check we needed to see some identification—like, say, a driver's license.

"We don't drive," Dr. Brown said.

"Do you have any credit cards?"

"We don't believe in them."

"A passport, maybe?"

"Of course," he said, as though everyone carried a passport. He had, in fact, five passports. I looked through them, noting that all the pictures were identical and all the names were different.

"Why do these passports all have different names?" I asked politely.

"I'm doing a little work for *the Agency*," he said, looking around to see who was listening. "You know."

I pretended that I "knew" and went to confer with the receptionist. She had Byron on the phone, and I explained the situation to him. He wanted collateral. I called Dr. Brown over to the counter and asked if he had anything else to demonstrate his ability to pay for what would probably be a two- to three-thousand-dollar flight. He thought about it for a minute and then smiled. He did have something, he suddenly remembered. It was out in the *car*. He would be right back.

Dr. Brown came back with a bulging shopping bag, and I restrained myself from asking who had driven the car. He laid several plastic pages filled with coins on the counter, and looked at us expectantly.

"What exactly are these?" I asked, still attempting to be polite.

"Mexican gold pieces," he said. "Each one is an ounce. With gold at, what, three-fifty, figure out how many you need to cover the trip. You can FedEx them back to me."

I had the receptionist get Byron on the phone again, and he approved the gold pieces after making us bite into them to see if they were real. He wanted ten put in the safe in case the check bounced. The receptionist took them out of the plastic pages and gave the rest back to Dr. Brown. Dr. Brown stuffed them into his shopping bag.

I went outside to do a preflight inspection of the airplane, half-hoping I would find something glaringly wrong. I had very bad vibes about these passengers.

The airplane, however, seemed to be in perfect shape.

Dr. Brown and Bo had said they didn't have much luggage, but they came out with matching black leather totes and at least thirty overstuffed shopping bags.

"What's in those bags?" I asked, concerned about weight and balance.

"Just personal stuff," Dr. Brown answered. "Nothing you need to know about."

"I need to know about their weight."

"I'd guess about fifteen pounds each," Dr. Brown said, handing me a bag. I agreed, and calculated the weight and balance accordingly. Dr. Brown walked around the Seneca, kicking the tires and knocking on the wings. I watched out of the corner of my eye and made a mental note not to leave him alone near the airplane.

"Bo's never been in one of these little kites," Dr. Brown said. "She really wants to see the Golden Gate Bridge up close."

"We can fly over it on our way up the coast," I told him. The fog was starting to lift, so I figured we had a good chance of seeing it.

"We want to fly *under* it."

I sighed and explained to Dr. Brown that flying under the Golden Gate Bridge would violate every FAA regulation imaginable. I told him that I, and all the other pilots at our company, flew strictly by the book, and if he was dissatisfied in any way he could go elsewhere. If Golden Gate lost the business, at least no one could fault me for adhering to regulations.

"Good answer, babe," Dr. Brown said, patting me on the back. "I like my pilots to be law-abiding and humorless."

By the time Dale came sauntering across the ramp, carrying his flight bag and a can of Coke, Dr. Brown and Bo were comfortably seated in the airplane, and I was on the radio trying to get an air traffic control clearance to fly over the Golden Gate Bridge. Dale tossed his flight bag into the airplane, jumped into his seat, and nodded to the passengers.

"I want to talk to you," I mouthed. "About the . . . um . . ."—
I inclined my head in the direction of Dr. Brown and Bo—"payload."

"Let's go," he said, plugging in his headset. "We can talk in the
air."

"I want to talk *now*," I whispered. "Before we get in the air."

But the air traffic controller called back with our clearance, and
Dale told him we were ready, so I had no choice but to start the
engines.

As pilot in command, I chose to give Dale the first leg. Our
clearance allowed us to fly along the west side of the bay and over
the Golden Gate Bridge at or below three thousand feet. The fog
had burned off, and we had a good view of San Quentin prison.

"I spent ten years there," Dr. Brown announced. He had left his
seat and was standing in the little space between the two pilot seats.

"In what capacity?" I asked, scanning the area for traffic and
fearing the worst.

"Staff psychiatrist," he said. At least he hadn't been a prisoner—
if he was to be believed.

"How interesting," I said, looking at Dale.

But Dale was concentrating on flying as slowly as possible so we
could log more time.

"I think maybe you should stay in your seat until we get to a
safer altitude," I suggested to Dr. Brown. "It could be a little bumpy
down here."

Dr. Brown obediently returned to his seat and pointed out the
Golden Gate Bridge to Bo, who was beginning to turn green.

"Are you ready to head up the coast now?" I asked Dr. Brown.

He said they were, and I requested permission from air traffic control to climb. I closed the curtain that separated our seats from the rest of the airplane.

"Dale," I said quietly on the intercom, "this guy is a nutcase." And I told him all that had happened at the airport.

Dale shrugged. "It's still multiengine time."

"What do you think he has in the shopping bags?"

"Our job is just to fly the airplane."

We flew along in silence for the next half hour. Dale and I enjoyed, at best, a strained relationship. He had been at Golden Gate longer, but I had more total flight time, which made me senior to him. While he flight instructed and flew occasional single-engine charters, I flight instructed and flew most of the single- and all of the multiengine charters. I wasn't required to take a copilot on my charters, but I knew it was the only way for Dale to log multiengine time. Although Dale never said no to a flight, he resented being in my power and strove to outdo me in the actual flying.

"There's the airport," Dale said, beginning a descent. It had turned into a beautiful day, the coastline was spectacular, and my headache had responded to the aspirin. I thought maybe I would enjoy this flight after all.

I pulled back the curtains to tell the passengers that we were approaching the airport and saw Bo lying on the floor with her eyes closed. One sleeve of her jumpsuit was rolled up, and Dr. Brown was injecting something into her arm.

"Um, excuse me," I said. "The airport's just off to the right. We'll be landing in five minutes."

Dr. Brown looked up and smiled. "The sooner the better," he said, pointing to Bo.

"Is she all right? Do you want me to radio ahead for a doctor or something?" I kicked Dale. He glanced back, then resumed his descent, unconcerned.

"I *am* a doctor," Dr. Brown said. "Like I said, it's her first experience in a small plane. She's just nervous. This will help her relax."

"Okay," I said. "But you both need to be in your seats with your seat belts fastened for landing."

"Got it," Dr. Brown said.

Dale made a perfect landing and taxied to the parking area, where a stretch limousine was waiting. While he shut down the airplane, I opened the passenger door. Dr. Brown gently nudged Bo down the steps. She was unsteady, and I had to help her stand.

"We're on the ground now," I said.

She looked at me with unfocused eyes. Dr. Brown put an arm around her, told us they'd be a couple of hours, and disappeared into the car.

By the time we took off again, after six hours in the one-room building that made up the airport office/terminal, the sun was starting to set. Air traffic control cleared us to Santa Monica via the "shark route"—meaning over the water. It was more direct, and since we were in a twin-engine airplane, it was no big deal.

I climbed to nine thousand feet, synced the props, leaned the mixtures, and settled down for a three-hour flight. While I admired the view, Dale engaged in nonessential conversation with a new woman controller.

"I can't get my cellular phone to work," Dr. Brown announced, parting the curtain. "It must be the altitude. You have to go lower."

"I don't think air traffic control will let us do that," I said. "We're on an instrument clearance."

"But I need to make a call."

"In a few minutes we'll be past the mountains. Maybe you'll get better reception," I said.

"Humph," Dr. Brown muttered, going back to his seat.

"What was that all about?" Dale asked when his controller had to talk to another airplane.

"He thought his cellular phone wasn't working because we were too high."

"I'll call Susan and ask for lower."

"Susan?"

He pointed to the radio, but Susan called us first to say that we were leaving her sector and to switch frequencies. The next controller—a man—was unimpressed with Dale's voice, so Dale was forced to talk to me.

"There's this new commuter starting up in Fresno," he said. "I hear they're taking pilots with under a thousand hours."

"You should apply," I said. "Have you finished your résumé yet?" Dale was always talking about finding another job, but he never seemed to get around to updating his résumé.

"What about you?" he asked. "I thought you were gung ho to get a commuter job."

"I don't want to live in Fresno." It's true that I was happy living in San Francisco, but I would gladly move to Fresno if a commuter airline would hire me. The problem was that although I'd had interviews with most of the commuter airlines in California, I hadn't been offered jobs at any of them. One said I was too short, another said I was overeducated, a third said they had already hired a woman this year, and the fourth said because I didn't work on my own car, I didn't have the mechanical background they wanted.

"They might have a base in Bakersfield, too," Dale added.

"It's still the valley, still hot, and still filled with cul-de-sacs and two-car garages," I responded.

"You'll never get a job if you act like a snob."

"We'll see," I said. I didn't want to tell Dale that I did, in fact, have an interview lined up with that very commuter next week, along with interviews at two freight airlines. Dale didn't consider "padding" his logbook with multiengine hours a moral dilemma if, as he claimed, it would get him in the door of an airline's employment office. Since it was hard enough getting myself in the door with my legitimate hours, I didn't need any additional competition from him.

"I wonder how late the bars are open down in Phoenix," Dale mused. "I wouldn't mind meeting some of those blond, tan Arizona girls."

I sighed. "We won't even get to Santa Monica until after nine. God knows how long *they* will want to stay—at least a couple of hours. We'll be lucky if we get to Phoenix by dawn!" My headache was coming back with a vengeance, and the thought of flying all night was almost more than I could bear. Let alone the idea of going out if and when we got there.

"I wasn't inviting you," he said. "A guy doesn't go out to meet girls with another girl tagging along."

The radio was quiet, and we droned along without speaking, staring out our respective windows. The moon was rising, and it illuminated the fog as it lapped at the coast. California had to be one of the most beautiful places in the world to fly.

"Hi, kids!"

We both jumped. Dr. Brown was standing between our seats with his cellular phone again.

"What can we do for you?" Dale asked him.

"Nothing. Just came to see what you were up to." He was idly pulling up and down on his phone's antenna.

"We'll be there in fifty-five minutes," I said. I prided myself on accurate estimates of arrival time.

"Sounds good." I expected Dr. Brown to return to his seat, but he stayed where he was.

"How's Bo?" I asked.

"Sleeping peacefully," Dr. Brown said. I wondered if it was a drug-induced sleep. "Check out my phone." He dropped it in Dale's lap.

Dale looked it over with appropriate murmurs of admiration.

"Did you ever get it to work?" I asked.

"Nah," Dr. Brown said, taking it back. He had brought his leather tote up front with him, and he rummaged through it. He pulled out another plastic page of coins. "What do you think of my collection?"

"It's . . . impressive," I said.

"I used to collect coins," Dale said.

"Yeah? Then take one," Dr. Brown offered.

"You don't want to give away coins like that," Dale said, eyeing them greedily.

"Sure I do. Go ahead. Pick one out. I insist." So Dale picked out a coin and put it in his flight bag.

"Thanks," he said.

"I like to keep my pilots happy," Dr. Brown said.

Air traffic control wanted us to climb to a higher altitude, so I advanced the throttles and raised the nose.

"Guess what else I have in my bag," Dr. Brown said.

"I give up," Dale responded, clearly feeling indulgent toward Dr. Brown.

"This," Dr. Brown said, triumphantly. He held up a hand grenade.

I had never seen a hand grenade in my life, but Dr. Brown's black, cylindrical object with the texture of a pineapple certainly had me alert.

"What do you plan to use that for?" Dale asked. I admired his calm. I subtly moved my shaking hand to the transponder, the radio that was automatically sending our flight path and altitude to air traffic control radar screens, ready to send the hijack code.

"You never know in my line of work," Dr. Brown said.

"Can I see it?" I asked, thinking that if I had possession, maybe I could somehow get rid of it.

"Sorry," Dr. Brown said. "It's mine."

"You realize that we *all* die if that thing goes off, right?" Dale asked.

"Of course," Dr. Brown said, hurt. "What do you take me for?" With that he took his tote bag and went back to his seat. Dale and I looked at each other.

"Would you call this a hijacking?" I asked Dale, my hand still on the transponder.

"He didn't ask us to take him anywhere," Dale said. "For all we know, it isn't even real. I think we should just pretend it didn't happen."

"How far is it to Mexico?" Dr. Brown asked, suddenly between us again. I was beginning to get, in pilot understatement language, concerned.

"A couple of hours," Dale said.

"We would have to stop for fuel first," I added, remembering a stalling tactic from an article I'd read about hijacking.

"Just wondering," Dr. Brown said, returning to his seat.

"Now would you call it hijacking?" I asked.

"He still didn't *demand* to go anywhere," Dale replied.

"I'm not going to Mexico with that maniac," I stated.

"Of course not," Dale said. "But think of how many hours we'd log if we did."

"We should tell the controller," I said.

"What are you going to tell him?" Dale asked. "That our passengers have a hand grenade?"

"Yes."

"But they haven't threatened us, have they?"

"I think the FAA would expect us to land at the nearest airport. Santa Barbara is right down there."

"Great," Dale said, sarcastically. "What do we tell the payload?" He gestured toward the back of the airplane.

"They'll think we're in Santa Monica," I said.

"You just told them it would be another fifty-five minutes. They can probably tell the difference between five and fifty-five minutes."

"We'll tell them there were good tailwinds—"

"We have to go to the bathroom," Dr. Brown said, swooping down on us once again.

"Santa Barbara is right down there," I suggested.

"Or it's only another forty minutes to Santa Monica," Dale added.

"Santa Barbara would be fine. Take us to that little restaurant with the good cheesecake."

"Okay," I said with relief. "We'll get permission to descend. You better fasten your seat belts."

Dr. Brown went back to his seat, and Dale told the controller we wanted to divert to Santa Barbara.

"Are you having any problems?" the controller asked.

"Yes—" I started to answer, but Dale cut me off.

"The passengers just want to make a pit stop," he said to the controller. "Watch your heading," he said to me. "We're off twenty degrees."

"Report the airport in sight for a visual approach," the controller responded.

I started a descent and tuned the radios for Santa Barbara. "We'll get rid of them here," I said.

"What do you mean?" Dale asked.

"I mean, we'll put them out. End of charter. They can take their stupid shopping bags and find another airplane to take them to Phoenix."

"If we do that, we'll lose the rest of the multiengine time," Dale complained. "So far today we've only flown five hours. We can't expect more than two and a half back. Do you want to give up ten hours?"

"If we're dead, the hours won't do us any good."

"I think you're overreacting. Even if it is a real hand grenade, I'm sure old Doc doesn't want to blow himself up."

I made a less than beautiful landing in Santa Barbara, but at least we were on the ground.

"Are you trying to activate the grenade?" Dale snickered.

I chose not to respond and taxied over to the transient parking area. I shut down the engines while Dale helped Dr. Brown and Bo out. They were taking their tote bags with them, I noticed.

"We need an approximate takeoff time so we can file a flight plan," Dale told them.

"Why don't we say an hour?" Dr. Brown said, putting his arm around Bo. "We'll just use the facilities and have a bite to eat."

They walked off toward the restaurant, and I crawled into the baggage compartment with my flashlight to get a look at the shopping bags. I found more coins, clothes, golf balls, and groceries. Ordinary things like ketchup in red plastic bottles, jars of peanut butter, cans of Parmesan cheese, two-liter bottles of Diet Coke. I had no idea why they would be carrying around ordinary groceries that they could buy anywhere.

"What are you doing?" Dale asked.

"What does it look like?"

"It looks like you're trying to steal something."

I closed up the baggage compartment and entered the passenger cabin.

"I'm just straightening up," I said, searching under the seats and in the seat pockets for needles and hand grenades. I found only empty yogurt containers, potato-chip bags, and soda cans.

"Discover anything?" Dale asked as I joined him leaning against the side of the airplane.

"No."

"I didn't think you would," he said with a smile.

"We need to decide what we're going to do with them," I began. "I'm not getting back in the airplane with a hand grenade."

"Fine," Dale said. "You're the captain. You can explain to Dr. Brown."

"Okay. I will."

But when Dr. Brown came back to the airplane, there wasn't an opportunity.

"You're going to have to go get Bo, babe," Dr. Brown said to me. "She's in the little girls' room. Hurry, hurry! We want to be in Santa Monica by eleven."

There was no way we would be in Santa Monica by eleven, I

calculated, walking to the restaurant. It was already after ten. But if we took off by ten-thirty and landed straight in, maybe we could make it by eleven-fifteen . . . if we agreed to take them, that is.

The restaurant was packed. It was a hangout for UCSB students, and apparently a lot of them hadn't gone home for Easter. I pushed my way through the bar in search of the women's room. When I finally found it, there was a line extending out the door. I jostled my way through only to find that Bo wasn't inside.

It wasn't my problem, I decided. I was the pilot, not the baby-sitter. Dr. Brown could find Bo himself. In fact, he could unload all his shopping bags and spend the rest of the night looking for Bo. Dale and I were taking the Seneca home.

As I headed out the door, I passed an alcove with a couch and several pay phones. Bo was on the couch with her arms wrapped around her knees, crying. "Bo?"

She looked up. "I thought he left me," she stuttered, pulling a tissue out of her tote bag.

"He thought you were in the bathroom," I said. "He sent me in here to find you."

"He told me to wait right here while he made a phone call," she said, apparently confused. "I don't know what happened."

"Well, are you ready to go now?" I asked.

"I guess," she said, blowing her nose. "He really didn't leave me?"

"Not unless he and Dale took off without both of us."

"I'm so happy," she said, smiling. "I would have been totally despondent."

We left the restaurant and walked back toward the airplane.

"Can I ask you a question?" I began while we were still out of earshot of the airplane.

"Sure."

"Do you know anything about that hand grenade he showed us?"

"Not really. Maybe it was a toy. He has a lot of toys."

"What does he do with them?"

"Nothing much. He just likes to scare people."

If this guy was really a psychiatrist, I felt very sorry for his patients.

"Honeybunch!" Dr. Brown called, running to meet Bo. He put his arm around her and propelled her toward the airplane. "I was so worried."

"But you told me to wait by the phones—"

"Shh. We'll be home soon." Dr. Brown helped Bo back into the airplane. "Okay, kids. Let's go. Up and away."

I climbed into the airplane. Dale had already picked up a clearance and was ready to go.

"I guess we're going to Santa Monica," he said as we started the engines.

"Bo said the grenade was probably fake. She said he likes to scare people."

"I told you," Dale said.

It was his turn to fly, so I handled the radios. We took off and were cleared direct to Santa Monica. I calculated that we would get there at eleven-thirty.

"Excuse me, kids," Dr. Brown said, parting the curtain. He seemed a little less peppy. I hoped that was a good sign. "We're going to skip Phoenix on this trip. Bo is a little tired. And we want to go to Orange County instead of Santa Monica."

Orange County was not far from Santa Monica, but it involved changing our clearance, getting out new charts, and retuning the radios. I took care of everything while Dale grumbled.

"We're losing out on at least six hours of flying time," he said.

"This guy is a jerk. He said he wanted to go to Phoenix, so he should go. He has no right to change his plans in the middle of the trip."

"The guy is a lunatic," I said. "He has five different passports, all kinds of drugs, and a hand grenade. He drives us crazy while we're flying, and he takes forever on the ground. I can't believe you want to fly even farther with him!"

"Think of your logbook. I was counting on at least sixteen hours."

"You're lucky you got any hours today. I almost canceled this trip as soon as I saw those people. If we get to Orange County alive, I plan to get their crap out of the airplane and check it completely before we take off again. I don't trust them at all."

Dr. Brown stayed in his seat for the rest of the flight, and Dale made another perfect landing. We taxied to the general aviation terminal and shut down the engines. This time, Dr. Brown let himself out before we could open the door for him. Bo followed.

"Good flight, kids," Dr. Brown said, handing Bo both totes. She started walking to the terminal. "Let's get the bags out, and then you can be on your way."

I opened the baggage compartment and started unloading the shopping bags.

"Bring them to the terminal, okay, babe?" Dr. Brown said to me, following Bo empty-handed.

"I'm not carrying these bags in for him," I told Dale. "That's not part of our job."

"But we might get a tip," Dale said.

"He already gave you that coin. You can carry his bags."

"Okay, but I get the tip."

"Fine," I said. "I don't care. I just want to get out of here."

It took Dale ten trips to get the shopping bags inside. Dr. Brown didn't give him a tip. He didn't even thank him. He just let Dale stack the shopping bags in a corner while he talked on the phone. While Dale was gone I searched the entire airplane, but again I found nothing.

Even though it should have been my turn to fly on the way back, I gave the leg to Dale. I was far too drained to enjoy it.

"He had a gun in one of those bags," Dale said, when we were halfway home. "A bag broke open and it fell out."

"Did it look real?" I asked.

"I don't know if it was loaded, but it definitely looked like the genuine article."

"What did you do with it?"

"I stuffed it into one of the other bags."

"We could have been killed," I said.

"If I'd known about the gun earlier—"

"You would have agreed to put them out in Santa Barbara?"

"Maybe . . ."

"So you think guns are more dangerous than hand grenades?"

"Look at the hours we got, though," Dale said, avoiding my question. "Someday, when we're airline pilots looking back through our old logbooks, we'll have great memories."

COMMUNICATIONS

B y the time I started flying for
Fast Freight, my mother had
launched a campaign to find
me a husband. I was already
twenty-five, she anguished. And she was turning sixty! Where were
her grandchildren? I was her only child (as if I could ever forget). It
was my *duty* to provide her with precious babies to love and spoil.
And whereas San Francisco wasn't *New York,* it still had cultural
resources through which I could meet suitable men. By taking courses,
for example (or, better yet, enrolling in graduate school). By going to
poetry readings and coffee houses. By joining a health club in the
financial district. Working on a political campaign. There were a
myriad of opportunities. If I would only expend the effort.

It wasn't that I was opposed to any of my mother's suggestions—
I wanted to someday fall in love, get married, and have children; it

was my lack of *time*. On weekdays my alarm went off at four-forty-five in the morning, and I didn't get home until after seven at night, by which time I was thoroughly exhausted. On weekends I still had a few students to teach at Golden Gate, where I was also on call as a backup charter pilot. My only opportunity for romance was on the radio in the airplane, and the air traffic controllers I talked to surely weren't what my mother had in mind as son-in-law/father-of-her-grandchildren material.

"Fast Freight one-twelve is with you, climbing out of a thousand," I announced in my most sultry radio voice when I was handed off to the southeast sector of Fresno Approach and Departure Control, the domain of my favorite controller.

"Good morning, Fast Freight one-twelve," he said in his deep, sexy, friendly California voice. "And how are you on this beautiful spring day?"

"Fine, thank you," I answered, although I would have been better if I worked for a different airline. I'd thought Fast Freight would be a step up from flight instructing and charter. After all, it provided steady pay (fifty dollars per day), consistent multiengine hours, and, on paper at least, was considered to be "airline" flying—meaning the flights were numbered, air traffic control clearances were filed by company dispatch, and uniforms were required. But $250 a week still barely covered my living expenses, the multiengine time only totaled 3.5 loggable hours per day, and although I finally had my blue epaulet shirt with four stripes on each shoulder, there weren't any passengers to see it.

"Do you have time for a question?" he asked.

"I always have time for you," I flirted.

"Any chance of ever bumming a ride back up to SFO?" For a

minute I allowed myself to fantasize what it would be like to have him in the seat next to me (the only other seat in the airplane—all the others had been removed to accommodate the cargo), sitting so close our shoulders touched, accidentally brushing his knee with my hand when I reached over to lean the mixtures. Was he tall and blond and tan from coaching Little League on his days off? Or did he have dark hair and circles under his blue eyes from controlling all day, going to law school evenings, and studying all night?

"I doubt it," I said regretfully. "The airplane is always filled to gross weight." Actually, I suspected that the airplane was always filled *beyond* gross weight. Fast Freight computed weight and balance based on volume rather than actual poundage. If the cargo compartment was full, the airplane would be considered at its maximum takeoff weight, regardless of whether it was filled with all heavy packages or all light ones.

"Couldn't hurt to ask," he said. "Contact Fresno on one twenty-seven seventy-five."

"Twenty-seven, seventy-five," I repeated. "Talk to you to-morrow."

"It's the high point of my day."

My route was from San Francisco to Visalia with a stop in Fresno. I reported to the airport at six in the morning, hand-loaded a thousand (or more) pounds of freight onto the airplane, and took off by seven. I landed in Fresno, unloaded half the freight, then flew on to Visalia, where I arrived by eight-thirty, unloaded the rest of the freight, tied down the airplane, and met up with the three other pilots who would be spending the rest of the day (until we reloaded at three-thirty) at the company apartment.

"It took you long enough to taxi," Wayne, one of the pilots, said as I got into the car where he and the two others, Willie and Julie, were waiting. The car, a beat-up Chevrolet Impala with starter problems, was provided by Fast Freight so we could get from the airport to the apartment.

"That's because I lost the right brake," I said. Fast Freight's maintenance policy was to not fix anything until it broke. Which meant something broke on every flight. The failure of the right brake hadn't been catastrophic, but it had forced me to taxi slowly enough to avoid using the left brake, which, applied by itself, would have either flipped the airplane over or put it into a continuous left turn.

But taxiing slowly had meant an overall decrease in bonus points for all the pilots at the company. Bonus points were the great motivator at Fast Freight. For every minute a pilot arrived earlier than scheduled, two points were added to the bonus bank. For every minute late, a point was subtracted. At the end of the month all the points were tallied up and converted to a monetary figure based on the company's profit for that period. The money was then distributed evenly among the pilots. In a good month, each pilot could make up to a hundred dollars from bonus points. Which, considering our pitiful salaries, amounted to a hefty increase.

"I've had it with my paycheck being dependent on their incompetent maintenance!" Wayne said, slamming his fist against the dashboard. "This is the last straw!"

Julie and I looked at each other and rolled our eyes. Every morning Wayne said he was going to quit, but the next day he was always back. Wayne worked as a security guard for a jewelry store at night and lived out of his car. The Fast Freight job not only provided him with additional income, it also gave him a place to sleep and shower during the day.

"We've *all* had it with this company," Julie said. "But we don't *all* bitch and moan incessantly." Julie had over three thousand hours (half of which were multiengine), and she was flying for Fast Freight only because the commuter airline where she'd been had gone out of business at a time when she hadn't had applications out with any of the major airlines.

"No bickering, children," Willie chided, backing the car into our assigned parking place in the apartment complex. "Or Uncle Willie won't make breakfast."

After Wayne had gone to bed and Willie had begun cooking, Julie and I got out our airline applications and sat down in the mismatched chairs at the chipped Formica table.

"They want to know my hobbies," Julie said, taking the cap off her pen. "But I don't really have any."

"Make some up," I suggested without looking up from the envelopes I was addressing to every commuter, regional, and major airline in the country. There were almost a hundred such airlines, and I rationalized that, even if I had only a one percent chance of being hired, as long as I applied to all of them, one would offer me a job.

"How about running, swimming, weight lifting—"

"Weight lifting?" I asked. Julie was five feet tall and couldn't have weighed more than ninety-five pounds.

"All that cargo we load and unload is *weight*," she said. "Then there's photography, gardening, and refinishing furniture."

"I didn't know you refinish furniture," Willie said, beating egg whites with a wire whisk. "I have this old dresser from my grandfather that I'd like to restore someday—"

"I don't *really* refinish furniture," Julie said. "But I've seen it done, so I could probably talk about it if I had to."

"I don't understand why you two want to work for the airlines,"

Willie said, ladling batter into his professional-quality Belgian waffle iron. Willie wasn't satisfied with the few pots and pans in the apartment, so he brought most of his cooking equipment from home. "They're so rigid and militaristic."

"We want to fly big airplanes," I said.

"And have decent schedules," Julie added.

"And get paid above the minimum wage," I continued.

"You won't like it," he told us, slicing fresh peaches to go on our waffles. "You'll miss my breakfasts and having your days off to sit at the pool."

"Maybe your breakfasts," 1 said.

"But not all the boring days at the pool," Julie said.

Our apartment was in a run-down building called The Flamingo, which had, as its only redeeming feature, a pool in the shape of a flamingo. Every morning after breakfast, for lack of anything better to do, Willie, Julie, and I went down to the pool.

"I think I'm in love," I told Julie from my perch on the steps of the pool (the flamingo's tail feathers) where I'd been reading one of the five or so novels I consumed each week.

"Anyone I know?" she asked from the raft she'd rescued from the building's Dumpster.

"I doubt it," I said. "He's the controller on one twenty-four six." Julie flew to Visalia from Los Angeles via Bakersfield, so she talked to different air traffic controllers.

"Is he in love with you, too?" she asked.

"He asked if he could have a ride to SFO."

"Probably because he doesn't want to drive," Willie commented from the lounge chair where he was working on his tan. Willie took his tanning very seriously. He wore a G-string bathing suit and tied a bandanna around his highlighted hair to keep it from being bleached by the sun. He repositioned himself to be facing directly into the sun every time its angle shifted, and he programmed the alarm on his watch to go off every thirty minutes so he could roll his body a quarter turn.

"I don't know," I said. "If all he wanted was a ride to San Francisco, I'm sure he could do better than Fast Freight."

"He must really want to meet you badly," Julie said, paddling her raft over to the tail feathers and joining me on the steps. "At least it gives you something to look forward to in the mornings."

"How's that turbulence?" my controller asked the next morning.

"Fine," I said through rattling teeth. One of the engines had suddenly started to vibrate, and I was trying different power settings to see if it would smooth out.

"It sounds like you're really bouncing around up there," he said. "Do you want to try five thousand?"

"It's not the altitude." I adjusted the propeller pitch controls to see if that would help.

"Are you having any mechanical problems?" he asked with concern.

"No." There was no such thing as a mechanical problem on a Fast Freight flight if the engines were still running and the airplane was in the air.

"Why don't you give me a call when you get on the ground?" he suggested.

"Am I in trouble?" Controllers didn't ask a pilot to call them unless the pilot had done something wrong.

"Not at all," he said, giving me the phone number of the radar room.

"I don't know your name," I said.

"Ask for L. J."

"He gave me his phone number," I told Julie as we were changing out of our uniforms.

"At home?" she asked.

"At work," I said, hanging my clothes on the shower rod. The apartment had only one closet, and it was in the bedroom where Wayne was sleeping. "He told me to call when I got on the ground."

"What are you waiting for?" Julie asked. "Go call him."

"Okay, okay." I carried the phone over to the ratty, cushionless couch. I was nervous and excited at the same time.

While I was dialing, Julie sat down at the opposite end of the couch with the newspaper. "I'm not listening," she said.

"Neither am I," Willie called from the kitchen, where he was preparing a Dutch apple pancake.

The phone was answered on the first ring, and I asked to speak to L. J.

"Are you all right?" he asked, picking up. His voice sounded just as good on the telephone.

"I'm fine," I answered. "Why?"

"I was worried," he said. "I didn't like the sound of that vibration."

"That's why they call it Fast *Fright*."

"You're a lot braver than I am."

"I'm just trying to rack up some hours," I said.

"Listen," he said. "I was wondering if you wanted to get together."

"You mean other than bumming a ride to SFO?" I asked.

"I changed my mind about riding in one of Fast Freight's airplanes," he said, laughing. "But we could do something else."

"Unfortunately, I'm stuck here all day."

"I know," he said. "But I'm off tomorrow. I could drive down and we could have lunch."

"You'd come all the way to *Visalia* for lunch?" I asked.

Julie lowered the newspaper and raised her eyebrows.

"Invite him for brunch," Willie stage-whispered. "I'll make quiche and croissants."

"It's not that far," L. J. said. "And how else will I ever get to meet you?"

"But . . . there's not much to do around here," I stammered, as Julie swatted me with the newspaper. I couldn't exactly see L. J. joining us around the shabby pool. And I didn't know anywhere else to take him. As far as I could tell, Visalia was a city of strip malls and trailer parks.

"I'm sure we'll find something," he said. "I'll be there by eleven."

"What do you think he looks like?" I wondered aloud. Julie and I were taking a break from tanning under the umbrella and sipping Willie's homemade lemonade.

"Probably bald and fat," Willie said, rolling over on his lounge chair.

"Not with a voice like that," I said.

"You can't tell anything about the way a person looks from a voice," Willie said. "We did voice-changing exercises in one of my acting classes, and you'd be amazed at the beautiful sounds that could come out of the homeliest people." Willie was an aspiring actor who planned to quit flying the minute he got his first big break.

"I think it's romantic that he wants to meet you badly enough to come all the way to Visalia," Julie said, returning to her raft. "And even if he is bald and fat, you can always close your eyes and listen to his voice."

∞

The next morning I was too nervous to eat Willie's Norwegian omelette.

"Maybe this is a mistake," I said at the breakfast table. "What if we have nothing to talk about?"

"You can always tell flying stories," Willie said. "And he can always tell controller stories. At least you have something in common." A sentiment with which my mother's voice in my head completely disagreed. What was an air traffic controller except a video game player of the airspace? her voice asked. It certainly didn't take a brain, an education, or an appreciation of art and literature to play video games. In fact, as she'd learned from one of her doctoral students, whose dissertation was on the sociology of video arcades, there was an inverse relationship between intelligence and video game proficiency.

"Is that what you're wearing?" Julie asked, looking me over critically.

"What's wrong with it?" I was wearing my favorite denim shorts and a royal-blue sleeveless T-shirt. It was ninety-eight degrees out, and blue was my best color.

"Let's at least do something with your hair," she said. "You are going on a date."

"Okay," I consented. "But no mousse or hair spray." Julie was into big hair. She spent a lot of time with "volumizing" hair dryers, hot rollers, and curling irons.

"If you're not eating that omelette, I'll take it," Willie said. "I can't stand seeing my culinary art go to waste."

"It's good," I said, passing him my plate. "I'm just not very hungry."

"I understand," he said.

"I'll make you a nice, simple French braid," Julie said. "Just so you'll look a little more festive."

It was almost eleven, and Willie and Julie were still on the couch reading the newspaper cover to cover.

"Aren't you guys going to the pool?" I asked hopefully.

"Eventually," Willie said.

"But you're missing prime tanning rays." It would be awkward enough meeting L.J. without having them around to pass judgment.

"We want to check this guy out," Julie said.

"We want to make sure he's safe," Willie added.

"What are you—my parents?" I asked.

"We're the next best thing," Willie said.

"Come on, Kendra," Julie said. "Can't we just say hello? I'm dying to hear his voice."

The doorbell rang, and Julie and Willie smiled at each other.

I opened the door.

"Hi," he said. "I'm Lee." He wasn't bald or fat, but I hadn't been expecting curly red hair and freckles. He was actually quite attractive, but he just didn't have a redheaded voice.

"I'm Kendra," I said as he looked me over.

"I know," he said, smiling. "You look like you sound."

"Is that good or bad?" I asked.

"Definitely good," he said.

Willie and Julie walked across the room to where we were standing.

"These are my apartment mates," I said. "They want to make sure you can be trusted."

"I promise to have her back by three," Lee said.

"Better make it two-thirty," Julie said.

"Okay," he said. "Two-thirty, then."

∞

Lee said he knew a great spot for a picnic, so we stopped at a deli, picked up some food, and headed for the foothills. It seemed very strange to be in a car with a man I'd never met, but Lee was good at making conversation.

"How long have you been working for Fast Fright?" he asked.

"Three months," I said. "The first time I talked to you was my first day."

"I remember it well," he said, smiling. "It's not often we get the privilege of a new, sexy female voice. Jack, the guy who works one thirty-one seven, wanted to ask for your phone number that week."

"Really?" I had no idea what my voice sounded like on the radio.

"It's true," he said, turning off the road into a state forest parking lot. "But I told him you weren't his type."

"How did you know that?"

"For one thing, Jack's at least forty," Lee said, stopping the car under some trees. "And for another, his idea of fun is beer and bowling. You don't seem like the beer-and-bowling type."

"No," I agreed, opening my door. "Neither of those are high on my list."

Lee grabbed the bag of food and led me down a path to the shore of a river. We sat on side-by-side boulders, and he handed me my sandwich and drink.

"So, when are you leaving for the airlines?" he asked, unwrapping his sandwich. It was cool and pleasant by the river, and I wondered why Willie, Julie, and I had never taken the car and driven up here.

"As soon as they'll have me," I said.

"I guess Fast Freight isn't your ultimate career objective," he said.

"It's not even my *current* career objective," I said, taking a bite of my shredded-vegetable-and-sprout sandwich. It was pretty good. Even the dumpiest delis in California, I'd learned, made decent vegetable sandwiches.

"I've heard alarming rumors about their maintenance," Lee said.

"It's more like *lack* of maintenance."

"Don't you think that's dangerous?"

"Nothing too terrible has ever happened," I said.

"Yet," he added.

"So how long have you been a controller?" I asked, changing the subject.

"Five years," he said. "I majored in psychology at Stanford, but I didn't know what I wanted to do with my degree. I've always been good at spatial relationships, and I work well under pressure, so I thought I'd take the test and see what happened. Every once in a while I think about graduate school, but I'm still not sure what field I want to go into."

Ha, ha, I told my mother's voice. You're wrong.

"Tell me everything," Julie said, as we were loading cargo into our airplanes that afternoon. "What was he like?"

"He was nice," I said. "He went to Stanford."

"Are you going to see him again?"

"I don't know yet," I said. "He lives in Fresno, and I live in San Francisco. The logistics are complicated."

"I missed you at the pool," Julie said. "Willie was studying a script for some audition, so there was no one to talk to. I hope your controller doesn't have too many weekdays off."

The next day, due to a brisk tailwind, I landed in Fresno ten minutes early. I helped the van driver unload the freight, saving another five minutes, and took off a full fifteen minutes ahead of schedule.

"Fast Freight one-twelve is climbing out of nine hundred for three thousand," I announced when the tower switched me to Lee's frequency.

"Recycle your transponder, Fast Freight one-twelve," Lee said. "I'm not getting you on the radar."

I recycled the transponder, but Lee still couldn't pick it up.

"Maintain three thousand," he said. "Report Visalia in sight."

"Climbing to three," I acknowledged.

"Yesterday was fun," Lee said. I heard whistles and catcalls in the background.

"We'll have to do it again sometime," I said. "I've got Visalia in sight."

"I'm off on Sunday," Lee said. "I'll give you a call tonight to set something up. Contact Visalia on one twenty-three zero."

Visalia didn't have a control tower; there was just a common frequency for local traffic to report their positions. I announced that I was entering left downwind for runway three-zero and turned parallel to the runway. I could see Wayne unloading his cargo, but it looked like I'd beaten Julie and Willie. I checked my watch. Seventeen minutes ahead of schedule, the earliest I'd ever been.

Abeam the end of the runway, I reduced power and lowered the landing gear. Wayne was going to be happy to see me today, I thought. Seventeen minutes amounted to a lot of bonus points.

It was quiet and peaceful in the airplane, and the hazy sun coming in the windshield felt warm and comforting. Willie was going to make another delicious breakfast, and Lee was going to call me tonight. I was so content it didn't immediately register that the quiet was because both engines had stopped running.

Suddenly the sun was not warm and comfortable, but overly bright and stifling. Sweat oozed out of every pore in my body, as I turned toward the runway and automatically went through the troubleshooting procedure—nothing from which improved the situation. As long as I stayed close enough, though, I would make the runway.

"Fast Freight one-twelve is turning left base," I declared on the radio to anyone who might be listening. "Negative engines."

No one responded, and I turned final high and fast. I wound up having to put the airplane into a slip to get it down, but I landed safely, right on the numbers.

The problem was that the airplane rolled out and came to a stop in the middle of Visalia's only runway. I tried restarting the engines, but neither would start. I announced my plight on the radio, but again no one answered. Finally, I had no choice but to get the tow bar out and start pulling. I prayed no one would land while I was still on the runway.

Just as I got the airplane clear, Julie touched down, followed by Willie. As they taxied past I saw them glance at me curiously, but I motioned them to keep going. We would lose too many bonus points if they didn't unload on time.

Unfortunately, Fast Freight's parking and unloading area was at the far end of the mile-long runway. I still had half a mile to go, and the airplane was heavy. I hoped Julie and Willie would send help, but I kept towing, just in case.

By the time Julie, Willie, and Wayne arrived in the car, followed by a mechanic with a tractor, I was not only soaked with sweat, but also had huge blisters on my hands and sore muscles in my arms, back, and neck.

"What happened?" Willie asked.

"I reduced power on downwind," I said, trying to catch my breath, "and both engines quit."

"Are you okay?" Julie asked.

"Just tired," I said, writing up the malfunctions for the mechanic. "And angry and frustrated."

"How much of a delay did you wind up with?" Wayne asked.

"I can't believe you, Wayne," Julie said. "Kendra almost got killed, and you're worried about stupid bonus points!"

"She didn't almost get killed," Wayne said. "And bonus points affect all of us."

"Actually," I said, "I landed seventeen minutes ahead of schedule. But I don't know how they're going to count the half hour it took me to tow the airplane." In order to earn bonus points, you had to arrive on the ramp—as opposed to the runway—ahead of schedule.

"I've had it with this company!" Wayne yelled, pounding the dash. "This time I've really and truly had it!"

"Either quit today, Wayne," Julie said, "or shut up!"

"I think I will quit," Wayne said. "Why should I put up with this crap one more day?"

After I'd changed and eaten two helpings of Willie's challah French toast, I felt a little better. I had survived a double engine-failure. I had brought the airplane and the freight down safely, without panicking. I was fairly proud of myself.

"I got offered a job," Julie said, as we walked down to the pool.

"What kind of job?" I asked. "Why didn't you tell me right away?"

"I'm not sure if I'm going to take it," she said. "It's with this corporation out of Santa Barbara. They have a Falcon and a Citation."

"It sounds great!" I said, hugging her. "You wanted to stay in southern California."

"It's only thirty hours a month," she said, sitting down under the umbrella. It was too hot to sit in the sun. "And the copilot doubles as the flight attendant. I didn't work this hard and log this many hours to serve coffee, tea, and little sandwiches."

"But it's jet time," I said. "The airlines will love it."

"And there's a training contract," she said, shuffling a deck of cards. "If you leave before you've been there two years, you have to reimburse them ten thousand dollars for your training. What if United or Northwest calls and I'm bound to the training contract? I want to be an airline pilot, not a corporate pilot." She dealt us a hand for rummy five hundred (or, in our case, because we had the whole day to kill, rummy five thousand).

"I'd take it," I said, arranging my cards. "I'd take almost anything to get out of here. After this morning, especially. I'm tired of imperiling my life in these airplanes! It's not worth it."

When we went back up to the apartment to shower and change, Wayne was sitting at the table studying his bank statements.

"Maintenance called," he said. "They fixed the engines, but the transponder is shot. Dispatch is going to notify Bay Approach." San Francisco's airport was in airspace that required a transponder, but with the advance permission of approach control, it was possible to land there without one.

"I'm not flying into San Francisco without a transponder," I said.

"Why not?" Willie asked, packing his frying pan in his flight bag.

"I'm not flying broken airplanes anymore," I said.

"Way to tell those bastards!" Wayne said.

"A broken transponder isn't a broken airplane," Willie said. "This week alone you've flown airplanes without brakes, with severe vibrations, and even with failed engines. And now you're saying you won't fly an airplane with a broken transponder?"

"That's right," I said. "The Bay Area has some of the busiest airspace in the world. I'm not taking any more risks for this company."

"How will you get home?" Julie asked, coming out of the bathroom with her curling iron. Willie took his towel and went into the bathroom, shaking his head.

"I guess I'll rent a car at the airport," I said.

"Does that mean you're quitting?" she asked.

"I'll have to," I said. "Otherwise they'll fire me."

"I'm quitting, too," Wayne said, holding up his bank statement. "I finally have enough money."

"Enough money for what?" Julie and I asked in unison. We knew Wayne hoarded his money, but he'd never told us why.

"To buy my airplane," he said. "A P-51 Mustang. I'm going to fly it around the world."

"Today's your last day?" I asked.

"Well . . ." he said. "It might take a few months to finalize everything . . ."

Julie and I looked at each other. Wayne would never quit.

Willie came out of the bathroom, and I went in.

I had no regrets about leaving Fast Freight, I ruminated as the water pounded on my sore muscles. Fast Freight was a miserable company. Their airplanes weren't safe. Their weight and balance procedures were bogus. Their schedules were inhumane. The idea of scrambling for bonus points was ridiculous. And without Julie (who

I knew would take the job in Santa Barbara), the days in Visalia would be unbearable. It would be a long drive home, and I would miss talking to Lee on the radio in the mornings, but anything was better than taking my chances in their airplanes again.

"You haven't called them yet, have you?" Willie asked me from the driver's seat as Julie and Wayne pushed the car (which wouldn't start) out of the parking space. I was too tired to push another one of Fast Freight's vehicles.

"No," I said. "I'm going to call from the airport."

"Good," Willie said, popping the clutch. The car started, and Julie and Wayne jumped into the backseat. "At least look over the airplane. I'm not saying you should fly it if you don't think it's safe, but you should at least make an effort."

"I have to get my flight bag out of it anyway," I said.

Willie parked the car at the airport, and the four of us walked across the ramp together. Our airplanes were tied down in the transient parking area, and they were the oldest, ugliest aircraft out there. Julie, Willie, and Wayne hustled through their walk-arounds and got their clearances so they would be ready to go as soon as the van delivered their cargo.

I stood staring at my airplane. The mustard-yellow-and-white paint had long ago faded and peeled. The fuselage was streaked with dirt. Old oil covered the engine cowlings. The wings were dotted with duct tape patches. I opened the door and saw my flight bag on the right seat. I noticed the yellow inoperative sticker on the transponder.

I heard the sound of the four vans racing across the ramp and the drivers simultaneously screeching to a stop beside the airplanes.

I heard the thump of boxes, bags, and envelopes hitting the ramp beside the cargo door.

I walked to the back of the airplane, still unsure of what I was going to do. But when the van driver dropped two coolers with URGENT DELIVERY—FRESH BLOOD stickers next to my door, I knew I had to fly the airplane back to San Francisco. I could always quit tomorrow.

APPROACHES

For the first two days of my annual summer visit to Princeton my mother's behavior was irreproachable. Norman was off at a conference, and she had booked a host of mother-daughter activities that included haircuts, facials, shopping, and the Metropolitan Museum of Art.

On the third day Norman returned, and when I came back from two hours of tennis at my old club, he and my mother were out on the back patio having drinks with a woman my mother introduced as Libby Neufelt, her good friend from graduate school. Libby, my mother explained, was a pioneer in the career-counseling field, and they'd been discussing the many career options available to a person with my talents and interests—such as technical writing, magazine editing, and library science. Libby, my mother added, had graciously offered to meet with me every morning for the rest of my stay to help me *focus* on what I might want to do with my life.

I thanked Libby for her offer and explained that I was happy in my current career.

On the fourth day my mother took me to lunch at the faculty club, where we ran into her dear friend Joanne, from the history department, and Joanne's husband, Bill. After we'd gotten a table for four, my mother revealed that Bill was a psychologist at Rutgers doing groundbreaking research on "the thrill-seeking personality" (motorcycle racers, mountain climbers, bungee jumpers, and lion tamers were the examples he used). My mother was sure Bill would be interested in pilots as well. And maybe after Bill had studied my thrill-seeking personality, he could refer me to an appropriate psychotherapist who could help me explore and overcome my attraction to danger.

I told Bill that I was afraid I wouldn't have anything to contribute to his research since flying was neither in the "dangerous" nor "thrill-seeking" category, but if I was ever in the market for a psychotherapist, I would certainly give him a call.

On the fifth day, I rented a car and departed (to my mother's dismay) to hand-deliver résumés and copies of my pilot certificates to every commuter and regional airline in New England. Since I hadn't found an airline job on the West Coast, I decided to try my luck in the East. Plus, Karen would be starting her pediatric residency at Boston Children's Hospital on July 1, and it would be great if we could continue to live together.

By the time I got to Providence, I had already been to eight different flight operations offices, none of which had yielded a chief pilot actually in residence. But at Northeast Connection I got lucky.

Not only was Chief Pilot Martin Wentworth Ashmont III there, but he invited me into his office.

"Why would a nice girl like you want to work for a bunch of ugly slimebags like us?" he asked, dumping a pile of outdated in-flight magazines off a chair for me to sit on.

"You're not that ugly," I said. Marty, as he'd introduced himself, looked like a young Paul Newman. He had silver-blond hair, a droopy mustache, and piercing blue eyes that stared at me relentlessly. If I hadn't been so nervous, I might have stared back.

"But I am a slimebag?" Marty asked.

"Um . . ." I stammered, not sure if this was a trick question, "I don't really know yet."

Marty laughed. "You're feisty," he said. "I like that in a girl."

I smiled tentatively. I couldn't tell if this was an interview or not.

"So why do you want to leave California?" he asked, opening a pack of honey-roasted peanuts and pouring some into his mouth.

"I want to fly for an airline, and there are better opportunities in the East," I said. "I've been sending you updated résumés every month—"

"Résumés have a way of disappearing around here," he interrupted. "Especially résumés that aren't local. There's no point in flying some guy out from California, putting him up, interviewing him, giving him a flight check, and then having him decide that the weather and women are fairer in California." He smiled meaningfully. "And California women *are* the fairest of them all."

"I didn't move to California until after college," I said, wanting to be consistent with my résumé.

"But you *look* like a California girl to me," he said. "And that's what counts."

There was a knock, and the door was opened by a man who, in

contrast to Marty's polo shirt and jeans, was wearing a genuine pilot uniform.

"Cliff!" Marty called out, winking at me. "Come interview our California girl."

Cliff was small and trim, with short dark hair and thick glasses. He handed Marty a stack of papers.

"Cliff is our assistant chief pilot," Marty said, absently signing the papers. "He does all the interviewing and hiring."

"Do you have a résumé?" Cliff asked.

I pulled one out of my backpack, conscious of the fact that in my shorts and T-shirt I was hardly dressed for an interview. (I'd given up on interview clothes after the third airline's chief pilot hadn't been available.)

While Cliff was reading my résumé Marty's right foot was inching its way under the desk. It was clad in a Birkenstock sandal, had neatly trimmed toenails, and was covered with curly blond hair. It came to rest alarmingly near my left foot.

"How much experience do you have flying in snow and ice?" Cliff asked, looking up from my résumé.

"I learned to fly in Hartford," I began, attempting to project confidence. But the fact of the matter was that, with the exception of my first fifty hours, all my flying had been in California, where the weather was mild and predictable. I'd never experienced in-flight icing conditions, and the only snow I'd encountered while flying had been on the side of the runway in Tahoe.

Cliff shook his head. "You don't have any turboprop time."

"But I have almost five hundred multiengine hours," I countered, as Marty's left foot followed his right, trapping my left leg between his ankles.

"Our insurance requires captains to have a thousand hours of multiengine time and at least five hundred of turbine time," Cliff said, unaware of the unfolding drama beneath Marty's desk.

"I happen to be an excellent pilot," I said, deciding to go for broke. I didn't have anything to lose. "I'm smooth and steady. I'm smart and efficient. I make amazing landings—"

"I have no doubt that you're a decent pilot," Cliff interrupted.

Marty smiled and moved his legs closer to my foot.

"I'm a good employee, too," I continued, telling myself not to think about those curly blond hairs tickling my calf. "Loyal, hardworking, responsible, punctual, dedicated—"

"I wish we could hire you," Cliff said sincerely. "You seem like a nice girl. But we're only hiring captains, and you just don't have the experience."

I looked at Marty.

He shrugged and retracted his legs.

"Well, thanks anyway," I said, standing up awkwardly. My foot had fallen asleep, and it was all I could do to keep from shaking it out.

"Feel free to try us again when you have some turbine time," Cliff said.

Marty waved from behind his desk.

I headed for the parking lot enveloped by despair, attempting to convince myself that each interview was good practice for the next. But at each interview it was the same old story. No one would hire me to fly a turboprop airplane without turboprop time. And how was I supposed to accumulate turboprop time if no one would hire me?

"Hey, California!"

I turned around.

Marty was standing in the doorway of the terminal. "We've got a class starting Monday morning at nine. You interested?"

"Sure," I said, striving not to seem too overjoyed.

"We're not supposed to be hiring copilots," Marty said, lowering his voice and motioning me closer. "And I don't want the word to get out, or we'll have every two-bit flight instructor on the East Coast banging on our door."

"My lips are sealed," I said, unable to keep from grinning like an idiot.

"But don't get too excited," he continued. "Because you're not *officially* hired until you pass your checkride."

"Do a lot of people fail?"

"Enough that you should be concerned."

I nodded. At least I'd have a chance. I couldn't ask for more than that.

"And California?"

I looked up.

"I hope you do make it through our training, because I'd like to see a lot more of you."

After four days of ground school (where I discovered that all seven of us—six men and me—had, in fact, been hired as Beechcraft 1900 *copilots*), I was scheduled to begin my flight training with Marty on Friday at midnight.

"Want a burger?" he asked, leading me out to the ramp, three hamburgers and a plate of french fries in one hand, two cans of soda in the other.

"No, thanks," I said, stifling a yawn. Flight training took place at night because the airplanes were in use all day.

Marty climbed the steps of a Beech 1900 Airliner, and I followed behind, surprised that he wasn't walking me through a preflight inspection of the 1900.

"Shouldn't I know how to do the preflight?" I asked.

"Your training captain will teach you," he said, consuming one hamburger in three bites and starting on the second. "Want some fries?"

I declined again, contemplating the inside of the airplane with awe. Although I'd been studying the 1900 manual all week, it hadn't prepared me for how *enormous* it would be. The biggest airplane I'd ever flown had six seats, including the two pilot seats. The 1900 had nineteen seats, *not* including the two pilot seats.

"We don't have a lot of time," Marty called from the left seat, where he was flipping switches with one hand and eating his third hamburger with the other. "Maintenance needs a few hours with this plane when we're done."

I dropped my flight bag behind the right seat and climbed over the throttle pedestal to get in. While Marty was starting the engines and dipping his fries in ketchup, I fumbled with my seat belt, which was comprised of five separate straps, all set too loose for me. By the time I got them adjusted, Marty had taxied us onto the runway.

The tower cleared us for takeoff, and Marty pushed the throttles forward. The airplane started rolling.

"Rotate at one-oh-five," he said, motioning for me to take the controls. "Climb out at one-forty." He leaned back in his seat and popped the top on one of his sodas.

We were halfway down the runway before I realized I couldn't reach the rudder pedals.

"You better take over," I said, trying not to sound panicky. We were nearing rotation speed. "I have to fix my seat."

"You can fix it in the air," Marty said, crushing his empty soda can and tossing it in the direction of his flight bag. "Rotate!"

I pulled back on the control wheel, and the 1900 leaped into the air. I tinkered with the pitch to maintain 140 knots, and Marty raised the landing gear.

"In the future you should get yourself organized *before* taxiing," he said, taking the controls so I could move my seat forward.

If he'd given me five minutes I could have, I wanted to say, but I was distracted by the vast array of instruments and gauges on the panel, only a few of which looked familiar.

"Head for Block Island and climb to ninety-five hundred," he said. "We'll start with air work."

At ninety-five hundred feet the sky was clear and the visibility was unrestricted, but below us, Marty complained (I was too busy getting used to the 1900 to look out my side window), the fog was starting to roll in.

While I went through the standard repertoire of stalls (in the 1900, to my relief, only *imminent* stalls were required), slow flight, and steep turns, Marty listened to the recorded weather for every airport in Connecticut and Rhode Island. The fog appeared to be moving quickly.

"Shit," he said, turning to a different frequency. "Damn. I guess we're going to have to go to Bradley for our approaches. It's the only place that's still clear."

At Bradley we worked on takeoffs and landings.

"You call that a landing?" Marty yelled, after I planted the airplane on the runway with a thud.

"Sorry," I said. It was one thing to take off and fly the 1900, but it was another thing entirely to land one. The 1900 was so much bigger than what I was used to that I was having trouble judging our distance above the ground and hence flaring too early.

"I thought you said you were good at landings," Marty said on our next trip around the pattern. "I won't be able to pass you if you can't show me at least a few decent ones."

"Pass me?" I asked, lowering the gear and flaps. I was only on my third landing in the 1900. I would hopefully have a lot more practice before my checkride, and I knew I would improve.

"This is a checkride, remember?"

"I thought this was a *lesson*," I said, finally guessing when to flare correctly. I looked over at Marty to see if he'd noticed my beautiful touchdown, but he was busy raising the flaps and pushing the throttles forward for another takeoff.

"We don't have time for *lessons*," he said. "We have a shortage of copilots in Boston, and I need you on the line tomorrow. Climb up to four thousand. I want to see your instrument procedures."

While I climbed, Marty asked approach control for a clearance to shoot the ILS to runway six. I hoped the controller would send us far enough out so I would have a chance to get the airplane stabilized, but he had us intercept the localizer just outside the outer marker. While I was scrambling to slow down, lower the landing gear, extend the flaps, and keep the localizer and glide slope needles centered, Marty decided to fail the left engine. I identified, verified, and pointed to the left propeller lever to simulate feathering it, but Marty apparently wanted the real thing because he did it himself. I was too busy trying to control the airplane to worry about the risk of shutting down a working engine at a low altitude. I somehow managed to get us over the runway at more or less the right speed, but then Marty decided we should go around.

"No way," I said, unable to believe I was arguing with the chief pilot on a checkride. But I'd heard that check pilots sometimes ask you to do something crazy just to see how you'll react. Well, I was going to react calmly, sanely, and safely. And the calm, sane, safe thing to do with a feathered engine and a long runway below the wheels was to land.

"Goddamnit!" Marty yelled, grabbing the controls. "I told you to go around!"

I let go and watched while he slowly pushed the power forward on the right engine and coaxed the airplane through a single-engine go-around. He gave it back to me for the landing, and I managed to put it down gently. I taxied off the runway, and Marty restarted the left engine.

"I wanted to show you this airplane *can* go around on one engine if it has to," he said. "Now let's go back to Providence."

I nodded, wiped the sweat off my face, and taxied back to the runway.

"So did you leave a trail of broken hearts back there in California?" Marty asked as we descended into the fog on our approach to Providence.

I shook my head, busy programming the approach frequencies into the radios.

"You mean to tell me that a pretty girl like you didn't have a boyfriend?" Marty asked.

"I was too busy flying," I answered, intercepting the approach course.

"Have you *ever* had a boyfriend?" I could feel Marty's eyes on me, even though my attention was on the instruments. "A *serious* boyfriend?"

"Gear down," I called.

"I hear that a lot of the girls in California like other girls," Marty said. "I can't say I blame them either."

The tower was reporting the weather right at minimums for our approach.

"It's guys who *only* like guys that I don't understand," Marty continued. "Who would want to sleep with a guy if he (or she) could sleep with a woman instead? A hundred feet to minimums."

It was bumpy in the clouds, and I was having trouble reading the instruments.

"Fifty feet," Marty called.

I felt sweat running down my back.

"Decision height."

Decision height without a report of the runway in sight meant we had to miss the approach. I started to push the throttles forward for a go-around.

"Approach lights in sight."

I reduced the power. Approach lights in sight authorized us to go down another hundred feet.

"Runway in sight."

I looked up and saw that we were over the runway. I pulled the power back and brought the nose up. We hit hard.

"Those landings of yours are pretty scary," Marty said, shutting down the engines at the maintenance hangar.

"I'm a little tired," I said. "It's two in the morning."

"Not much of a party girl, are you?" he commented, looking over at me. "I guess you're too tired even to celebrate passing your checkride."

"I passed?" I asked, having been so focused on flying that I'd completely forgotten I was taking a checkride. "You mean I can get excited?"

"You bet," Marty said, laughing. "I love seeing girls get excited."

He opened the door, and we climbed down the steps. The cool air felt wonderful on my face, and I smiled broadly as it slowly dawned on me that I was now a commuter airline pilot!

"We never finished our conversation," Marty said, as we walked across the ramp. "Did you have any serious *girlfriends* in California?"

It was Northeast Connection policy that all newly checked-out or upgraded pilots fly with a training captain for their first month on the line. I'd been assigned to fly with Nick, a thirty-eight-year-old, crew-cutted, ex-air traffic controller.

According to Nick, the copilot existed for only three reasons: to open and close the main cabin door, to make the PA announcements, and to fly should the captain be too hungover to do it himself. After two weeks as Nick's copilot I was a whiz on the PA, was making consistently decent landings (thanks to the fact that Nick was *always* hungover), but was still struggling with the door.

The door, which incorporated the steps by which all occupants of the airplane enplaned and deplaned, weighed at least a hundred pounds. From inside the airplane the only way to close the door was to pull it up using the two rubber-covered wires that acted as railings when the stairs were extended. This wasn't as easy as it sounded. Especially for a person who was five feet two inches tall and weighed only a little more than the door.

I had tried everything: standing and pulling on both railings, standing and pulling on one railing, kneeling and pulling on both railings, kneeling and pulling on one railing, sitting and pulling on both railings, sitting and pulling on one railing. Today I was trying a semicrouch and pulling on one railing. It had been successful for the day's first three legs, but on the fourth, my foot slipped on the carpet, and I wound up lying sprawled in the aisle with the door still open. A passenger in the front row took pity on me, unfastened his seat belt, and got up from his seat to help. Together we got the door closed easily.

"You're pathetic with that door," Nick said, shaking his head. "Marty must have hired you because you're a girl." He moved his eyes up and down my body. "A little underdeveloped, but otherwise not bad."

"Marty hired me because I'm a competent pilot," I told him.

"Believe whatever you want," Nick said, starting the engines.

I switched my microphone to PA and began briefing the passengers on the safety features of the airplane.

"I've got a splitting headache," Nick said after I'd finished. "And I have all this bullshit to read." He pulled a legal folder out of his flight bag. "If you know what's good for you, you won't bother me."

The good thing about Nick was that I got to fly almost every leg. The bad thing about Nick was that he had extreme mood swings.

The tower cleared us for takeoff. Nick acknowledged, and I pushed the throttles forward, checked the engine gauges to see that they were all within limits, and released the brakes. I loved the surge of power and the way the 1900 raced down the runway, building up speed. I loved the way it lifted off and soared into the sky. I loved the way the pressurization kept the cabin quiet and allowed us to climb at two thousand feet per minute. I loved everything about flying the 1900!

"NorCon five-zero-two, Boston Departure," I heard in my headset. NorCon was Northeast Connection's radio call sign. Five-zero-two was our flight number.

I looked over at Nick. It was company policy that the nonflying pilot work the radios, but Nick was reading and making no move to respond.

"NorCon five-zero-two, Boston Departure," the controller called again.

"Go ahead," I finally answered.

"NorCon five-zero-two, I've called you four times! Climb and maintain six thousand."

"Out of four for six," I said, establishing a climb.

"Listen up from now on, NorCon."

"Sorry," I said.

"Never apologize to a controller!" Nick bellowed, looking up from his folder.

"I didn't want us to get a violation," I said.

"That pansy-ass scab wasn't going to even think of giving us a violation!" he roared.

"But we missed an altitude—"

"You don't fucking say you're sorry! Jesus Christ! That gives those fucking power-hungry faggots a reason to write us up." He slammed his fist on the instrument panel. "You say your fucking radio wasn't working, so you switched to the other one. Got it?"

"Yes." There wasn't much point in arguing with Nick.

"It would be nice if I could have a little peace around here!"

On the ground in Burlington I helped the passengers disembark, gave operations our fuel load, computed the weight and balance, reviewed the new weather, helped the outbound passengers board, and closed the door without falling. I'd hoped Nick would notice my newfound proficiency, but he didn't look up from his reading until it was time to start the engines. And once they were started, he went back to his folder and didn't speak until we were fifteen minutes out of Manchester, where we'd be laying over.

"Goddamn lawyers," he muttered. "Blood-sucking leeches! All they do is send you papers to sign, and each time it costs you another five hundred bucks. I think those asshole lawyers invented divorce just to get money from hardworking stiffs like me."

I tuned the radio to Manchester's recorded weather information station and tried to copy down what they were saying, but Nick kept interrupting.

"The sooner I'm done with that dumb bitch, the better. She wants the house, the furniture, the cars, the kids! I'm the one who's been holding down a job all this time, but she gets everything! I ask you, is that justice?"

"I'm trying to get the weather," I said, holding up my hand for Nick to be quiet.

"You don't need to listen to that shit," he said, changing the frequency on the radio "You can see it's clear."

"I'd like to know where the wind is coming from," I said. "And it would be nice to have the temperature to tell the passengers."

"Just make it up," Nick said, switching to the PA. "Good evening, ladies and gentlemen, this is your captain. We'll be at the gate in Manchester in five minutes. Manchester weather is clear, the wind is out of the south, and the temperature is a balmy seventy degrees. We'd like to thank you for flying Northeast Connection, and we hope to see you on another one of our flights soon." He smiled at me with a look of smug satisfaction.

In the van on the way to the motel, Nick took off his tie, stripes, and company ID.

"It's almost Miller time," he announced, suddenly cheerful. "I can taste that first cold one going down right now!" He licked his lips in anticipation and then looked accusingly at my stripes. "You can't go into a bar in uniform."

"I'm not going into a bar," I said.

"I suppose you're a slam-clicker," he muttered.

"A what?" I asked. This was my first layover.

"As soon as you get into your room you *slam* the door and *click* the lock."

"It's already nine," I said. "And we have to be at the airport at six-thirty, which means getting up at five-thirty . . ."

Nick shook his head. "Better get those eight hours of sleep," he said. "We wouldn't want you to be a sleepy girl tomorrow, now would we? But it's part of my job as your training captain to let you know that it doesn't look good for the first officer not to have a friendly cocktail with the captain. It looks like the first officer isn't a team player. It looks like the first officer doesn't fit in. And first officers who don't fit in don't have much potential for advancement—if you get my drift."

"You've made yourself abundantly clear," I said as the van pulled into the motel parking lot.

I had taken a hot bath and just gotten into bed with my book when someone began banging on the door.

"Who is it?" I called.

"It's me," Nick said. "I need to talk to you for a minute. About our flight tomorrow."

I looked through the peephole and verified that it really was Nick. Maybe our departure time had been changed, I thought. Maybe we'd be flying a different route. Maybe maintenance was going to exchange our airplane.

As soon as I unlocked the door, Nick shoved it open. He pushed past me carrying a nearly empty bottle of Scotch and a black attaché case. He dove onto the bed and began bouncing up and down.

"What did you want to tell me about our flight?" I asked, standing by the open door.

"Hey, shut the door," he said. "I'm not gonna hurt ya."

"You're going to break the bed," I said, trying to remain calm and reasonable. "And it's going to be hard to explain what you were doing in my room that could have caused the bed to break."

"Sit down and talk to me for a minute," Nick crooned. He stopped bouncing and patted the blanket. "I'm lonely."

I left the door half-open and sat down in a chair as far from the bed as possible.

"Let me pour you a drink," he offered, opening up the attaché case, which contained a complete miniature bar. "You'd be a much happier person if you'd just relax a little."

"No thanks, and I think you've had enough," I said, calculating how late he could drink before becoming illegal to fly tomorrow's flight. The FAA regulation stipulated a minimum of eight hours "from bottle to throttle." If our flight was scheduled to depart at seven A.M., and it was almost ten-thirty now, he could legally drink for another half hour.

"Just one more itty-bitty sippy-wippy," Nick said, carefully measuring out a shot of Scotch and pouring it into one of the glasses from the attaché case. "All I need right now is a nice massage to soothe my aching muscles."

"Why don't you go back to your room and look in the phonebook for a masseuse?" I suggested.

"Come on, give old Nicky a massage," he said, taking off his shirt and rolling over onto his stomach.

"If you don't leave, I'll have to call the front desk." I reached for the phone, but Nick grabbed it first. He yanked it out from the wall and curled himself around it.

"Come and get it," he sang.

I got up and opened the door to the room all the way. Then, while he was still occupied with the phone, I grabbed the bottle of Scotch and the attaché case bar and ran for the door. Nick jumped up and lumbered after me.

"What are you doing with my bar?" he yelled indignantly. "Give it back!"

I left his bottle and attaché case outside his room. As he went running after it, I raced back into my room and slammed, clicked, and bolted the door.

"Hey, California!" Marty said, putting his arm around me as I entered operations the next day. "How's it going?" Nick and I had just landed in Boston. I'd flown all three legs while he'd silently consumed coffee and swallowed aspirin.

"I love flying the 1900," I said, deciding not to mention the layover.

"What do you think of our California girl, Nick?" Marty called, as Nick entered the room.

Nick stared at Marty's arm around my shoulder. "She can't close the goddamn door," he said.

"I had a little trouble at first," I said. "But now that I've figured out a good position—"

"Position is everything," Marty said, winking at me. He turned to Nick. "How are her landings?"

"Okay," Nick said. "But it's pretty damn unprofessional when the passengers have to help her with the door."

"She'll learn," Marty said, squeezing my shoulder. "Look how small she is! She needs to build up some muscles."

"Yeah, whatever," Nick muttered.

∞

On Monday morning Nick was in a good mood. Our schedule called for four round trips between Boston and White Plains, the first three of which I flew while Nick hummed along to an AM station he'd picked up off one of our navigation radios.

On the first leg of the last trip Nick decided to drum to the music using pens as drumsticks and the instrument panel as a drum. Halfway to White Plains, during an exuberant drumroll, one of the pens fell onto the floor on my side of the cockpit. Nick reached down to get it, then continued drumming.

Suddenly we flew into the clouds, and I was forced to shift my full attention to the instruments. While I navigated along the airway, Nick's pens began landing near my feet with increasing frequency.

"I'll get it," I said, reaching down the next time a pen hit my leg. I didn't want to reverse Nick's good mood, but it was difficult to hold the airplane on course and altitude when he kept blocking my view of the instruments.

"But I like groping between your legs," Nick said, reaching over.

"You're distracting me," I said.

"I'm flattered," he said, plucking the pen off the floor.

"It's not safe."

"What are you going to do about it?" He dropped both pens between my legs. "Tell your good friend Marty that I was *distracting* you with my hands between your legs?" He reached over to my side.

I pulled my legs up onto the seat until he'd retrieved his pens. The airplane hit turbulence and climbed five hundred feet. I lowered my legs to the floor and pushed the nose down. Again a pen fell onto my side. Again I pulled my legs onto the seat.

When we landed in White Plains I helped the passengers down the steps, then climbed back into the airplane. Between flights it was the first officer's job to straighten seat belts, return magazines to seat pockets, and remove trash. I always started in the back and worked my way forward. The Boston–White Plains route carried a business crowd who were generally neat. I needed only to straighten the seat belts and remove a few *Wall Street Journals* from the floor. I was thinking I might even have time to run into the terminal and buy something to eat when I noticed Nick sitting in the front row with his legs across the aisle, blocking my access to the door.

"I'm going to the café," I announced. "Do you want anything?"

"I want you to pay the toll before you leave," he said.

"Come on, Nick," I said. "We only have ten minutes."

"Either pay the toll or climb over."

If I had to scream for help, no one would hear, I suddenly realized. We were alone in the airplane and would be alone on the ramp until we radioed that we were ready to board the passengers.

"Please move your legs," I said.

"Don't you want to know what the toll is?" Nick asked, smiling menacingly. "A kiss. A teensy-weensy little kiss."

"Please move your legs," I repeated, starting to feel claustrophobic.

"No can do," he sang.

I *had* to get out of the airplane, and there seemed no choice but to climb over.

"You think you're too good for me, don't you?" Nick hissed, grabbing me on my way over his knees. I kicked and fought, but he trapped me astride his legs. "You're too busy screwing Marty, Mr. College Graduate Chief Pilot. But I have news for you, babe. I'm the one who makes or breaks your career at this airline. As your training captain, I can recommend that you be terminated. I can say you just don't have what it takes. How about that?" He released me, and I ran into the terminal.

"There you are," our agent said as I burst through the doors. "I've been trying to get you on the radio. We're ready to board."

"Not yet," I stuttered, pushing past her and charging for the women's room. I was trembling with rage, fear, and confusion. I couldn't think straight.

"What's going on?" she asked, following behind. "Are we taking a delay?"

"I don't know," I said, leaning against the wall.

"Is there a maintenance problem?"

I shook my head.

"I've got nineteen passengers waiting. I have to tell them something." She put her hands on her hips and waited for my response.

"Could you just leave me alone for a few minutes?" I asked.

"I'm putting this down as a pilot delay," she said, opening the door. "And you can explain it to the chief pilot yourself."

My heart was pounding, and I forced myself to breathe deeply. Nick had touched and threatened me. That was harassment. But what could I do? White Plains wasn't a crew base. There weren't any other copilots available to fly. If I refused to take the trip, the flight would be canceled, the airplane immobilized, and I'd still be stuck with Nick. I had to talk to someone.

I borrowed the ticket agent's phone and called the chief pilot's office.

"Marty's not in," the secretary said.

"Do you know when he'll be back?"

"He plays polo on Monday afternoons and usually doesn't come back to the office."

"Is Cliff there?" I asked.

"Cliff is flying."

"Is there anyone I can talk to?" I asked in desperation.

"Hold on," she said.

She connected me to the head of scheduling.

"What can I do for you?" he asked.

"I'm on a trip, and I'm having a problem with the captain," I said, turning my back to the agent.

"Finish the trip and make an appointment to see Marty," he said.

"I'm not sure it would be safe to finish the trip," I said, "given the situation."

"If you're calling in sick or incapacitated, you'll need to produce a note from a physician," the scheduler told me. "If you're stranding the airplane for any other reason—well, put it this way, it isn't going to bode well for your future at the company."

I hung up the phone and turned around. The passengers had clustered at the counter and were angrily demanding information about our departure. The agent gestured in my direction and shrugged.

I looked at my watch. We were only five minutes late. We could easily make up the time en route. I could make an appointment to see Marty tomorrow. "Go ahead and board," I told the agent.

On the last leg Nick flew, talked to air traffic control, and sang along with his AM station. I sat scrunched against my window, as far from him as I could get.

Back in Boston he was the first one out of the airplane. I waited for the passengers to leave, then grabbed my flight bag and headed into operations.

Boston operations consisted of two rooms. One housed radios, computers, and dispatchers; the other was a break room for pilots, baggage handlers, and fuelers. The only way to get from the ramp to the terminal was to walk through the break room.

Nick was at one of the tables with four baggage handlers. His attaché case bar was open, and a bottle of tequila was being circulated.

"Hey, babe," Nick called. "Wanna eat the worm?"

I headed for the door.

"If you want a good report from Captain Nick," he said, "you're gonna have to pay the toll." He laughed, the baggage handlers laughing with him. They each poured another drink and toasted one another.

I was almost to the door when Nick stood up on the table.

"The toll's increased," he said, unzipping his pants. "Better pay up."

I heard their laughter all the way to the parking lot.

"I'm having a little trouble flying with Nick," I told Marty. We were in his office, and I was sitting in the same chair I'd sat in during my interview less than a month ago.

"What kind of trouble?" he asked, kicking off his sandals and putting his feet up on the desk.

"I think he has a drinking problem," I said.

"That's a serious accusation," Marty said, looking uncomfortable.

I told him about our layover and Nick's portable bar and bottle of Scotch.

"But you didn't see him drink after eleven, did you?"

"No."

"And he didn't report to the airport drunk the next morning?"

"I couldn't tell, but he was drinking a lot of coffee and swallowing a lot of aspirin."

"Do you have absolute proof that he was drunk at flight time?"

Marty asked. "Can anyone back you up? Gate agents, baggage handlers, anyone?"

"I don't know," I said.

"It's a sensitive issue," Marty said. "You could be costing someone his license and livelihood."

"I think he also has a problem with women," I said.

"Now that's serious," Marty said, smiling and relaxing.

I explained how Nick had pushed his way into my room.

"But you opened the door. That could look like you *invited* him in."

I told Marty about the pens between my legs and the toll.

"He was just teasing you," Marty said, bringing his feet down and leaning forward in his seat. "Men tease women when they *like* them."

I told him how Nick had been drinking in operations and how he'd unzipped his pants on the table.

"He shouldn't have been drinking in uniform," Marty said. "I'll talk to him about that."

I sighed in frustration. "Nick also mentioned some nasty things about you and me," I said quietly.

"What!"

I finally had his attention. "He seems to think that—"

"I know what you're saying!" Marty yelled. "I just can't believe it. Jesus! I've never touched you. I can't let it get around that I'm screwing one of my female pilots. I'd never get another job!"

"I really love flying for Northeast Connection," I said. "And I don't want to make a big deal out of this, but Nick threatened that I could be fired—"

"Don't worry about it," Marty said absently.

"But I am worried about it. There are no grounds for me to be fired."

"You're not going to be fired, Kendra. I'm the chief pilot. I decide who gets fired around here."

"But Nick said—"

"Nick has absolutely no authority, okay?"

"Okay."

"I don't think you should fly with Nick anymore," Marty concluded. "I'll work something out with the scheduler about getting you another training captain."

"Thanks," I said, standing up to leave.

"I'd rather you didn't mention this to anyone," Marty said. "I'll talk to Nick myself."

I don't know if Marty ever talked to Nick or not, but a week later his name was gone from the pilot roster, and I heard a rumor that he'd lost his certificates for having too many DWIs.

SENIORITY

Now that I lived in Cambridge, my mother had taken to "dropping in" on a regular basis. It seemed there was always some academic function for her to attend at Harvard or Boston University, and she used those occasions to take me out to dinner and question another aspect of my career. This month it was Northeast Connection's uniforms, which, she asserted, not only looked like they'd come off the rack at Kmart, but illustrated in indisputable fashion (no pun intended) how women in male-dominated fields were forced to imitate men in order to survive.

And, as much as I'd wanted to dress like an airline pilot, I had to agree that our uniforms were atrocious. Both the men's and the women's were made of shiny blue polyester (white polyester for the shirts), but whereas the men's looked like most airline pilot uniforms, the women's looked like something Flight Attendant Barbie would wear. The jackets were lapel-less, buttonless, and cinched at the waist. The shirts had puffy sleeves and long strips of fabric around the collar for making into a bow at the neck. The slacks had neither belt loops nor pockets. And the hat was so horrible I'd never even unpacked it from its plastic wrapping.

It was my mother's idea to have a new uniform custom-made. She consulted her local birdies and presented me with the name of a good, yet reasonably priced, tailor in the North End. Fortunately Pam and Beth, the only other women based in Boston, were equally unhappy imitating Flight Attendant Barbie and had easily been recruited to participate in improving the image of NorCon's female pilots. The new uniforms were going to cost five hundred dollars each, the tailor explained on our first visit, but he assured us we would be happy with the final product. The fit would be flattering, the color would match the old uniforms exactly, and we had his word there wouldn't be so much as a thread of polyester.

"You come back for a fitting in two weeks," he said, writing down our measurements. "Maybe then you girls will be captains and I'll sew on the fourth stripe, yes?"

"Maybe," Beth said, checking her makeup in the tailor's mirror.

"But I wouldn't hold my breath," Pam added. "There aren't any woman captains at Northeast Connection."

"What do you mean, no woman captains?" the tailor asked. "You girls fly just as good as the boys, yes?"

"Better," Beth said.

"Then I don't understand," he said.

"Neither do we," I said.

We thanked the tailor and then walked across the street to Mike's Pastry Shop for cannoli.

"If they upgraded in seniority order, we'd all be captains," I said, as we sat down at a table by the window. Northeast Connection had 176 pilots, half of whom were captains. Beth had been with the airline for eighteen months and had a seniority number of 51. Pam's number was 72. And mine, after eight months, was 86.

"My dad said we need a union," Beth said, sipping her cappuccino. Beth's father was a 767 captain for Delta, active in ALPA, the Air Line Pilots Association.

"When I was hired," Pam said, starting on her third cannoli, "they said upgrade time was six months." Pam was tall and thin and could eat whatever she wanted without gaining a pound.

"They told me I'd upgrade as soon as I logged a thousand hours of turboprop time," Beth said.

"They told me I'd upgrade when I was *ready*," I said. "Which proves that there's no upgrade policy at all."

"If management doesn't want to upgrade certain pilots," Beth commented, "they just come up with excuses."

"It's total discrimination," Pam agreed.

"I think we should write a letter asking what the qualifications for captain are," I suggested. "Then, if we all meet them—which I'm sure we do—we'll write another letter asking for the reasons we're being passed over."

"My dad told me never to sign my name to any letters," Beth said. "He said they always find a way to use it against you."

"But Beth," I protested, "you're the one being hurt the most by this. You've been with NorCon longer than almost three-quarters of the pilots. They're hiring captains off the street who have less turboprop time than you do!"

"I know," Beth said. "And it really pisses me off. But if I get a reputation for being a troublemaker they'll never upgrade me."

∞

Gene was one of my favorite captains. He was in his early forties and had spent ten years flying jets for a corporation. When the corporation had disbanded its flight department, he'd applied to all the major airlines. But the major airlines, it seemed, were looking for younger pilots, and Gene had come to Northeast Connection.

"What's your seniority number?" I asked him on the way to Baltimore.

"Seventy-five," he answered. "Why?"

"That makes you junior to Pam and Beth," I said.

"True," he said. "Pam was in the class before mine, and Beth came from the merger with Yankee. Will you ask if we can have fourteen as a final? I want to stay out of the clouds."

I told the controller we wanted fourteen thousand as our final altitude, and he cleared us as requested.

"I wonder why they even bother with a seniority list," I commented.

"Have you ever heard of an airline *without* a seniority list?" Airline seniority traditionally governed everything from upgrades to base assignments to trip bidding, vacation, pay, and benefits.

"Most airlines *use* theirs," I said.

"I see what you're getting at," Gene said. "And you're right. Beth and Pam have paid their dues, and they deserve to be upgraded before any more captains are hired. On the other hand, when they started here they didn't have the time or experience to be captains."

"But now they have *more* time and experience than most of the new captains."

"Maybe," Gene said. "But you have to look at it from my point of view, too. I came here with five thousand hours of jet time. I'd been making sixty grand a year flying a G-II. I have a wife, two kids, car and mortgage payments. I couldn't *afford* to be a first officer." First officers were paid fourteen hundred dollars a month. Captains made three thousand. "If they hadn't hired me as a captain, I wouldn't have taken this job."

"That was a while ago," I countered. "But now things have stabilized, and the first officers who've been logging turboprop hours for the past six months should be given the opportunity to become captains."

"Sounds fair," Gene agreed. "But what can you do about it?"

"I'm thinking of writing a letter," I said.

"Good idea," Gene said. "I just hope it doesn't jeopardize *your* chances of upgrading."

"Did you hear the news?" Pam asked, modeling her new uniform for the tailor.

"Is it good or bad?" I came out of the dressing room and studied myself in the mirror. The new uniform was a vast improvement over the company's. The slacks were pleated and had belt loops and front pockets. The jacket had lapels and buttons, and it was roomy enough for a sweater underneath. The shirts were 100 percent cotton and had regular collars. The only thing we'd have to add would be navy blue ties.

"Very good," the tailor said, circling Pam and examining her critically. "Very nice. I'll just pin up the hem and you can have the whole thing next week."

"Beth goes to upgrade training on Monday," Pam said as the tailor finished pinning her pants.

"That's great," I said, changing places so he could inspect my uniform. "How did it happen?"

"That's the other news," Pam called from the dressing room.

"You know Jenson, that new vice president?" There was a new vice president in charge of flight operations, but I had yet to meet him. "Well, when he heard they were upgrading randomly, with no regard to seniority, he went ballistic and said the company could be sued."

"I wonder if he read my letter," I mused. I'd sent the letter to the chief pilot, but it could easily have found its way into Jenson's hands.

"You sent a letter?" Pam asked.

"A few weeks ago," I said. "But I never got an answer."

"You didn't put our names on it, did you?"

"Just mine." Although I'd discussed the seniority situation with most of the pilots in the Boston base, no one had been willing to sign it.

"Good," she said, coming out of the dressing room and handing the tailor her slacks. "I saw a copy of the training schedule, and I should be going to class in April."

"That means I should be going in May or June."

"Don't get your hopes up," Pam said, pulling a Heath bar out of her purse. "They still haven't decided what to do about the newest captains. They can't demote them, or they'll all quit. But if they upgrade the entire top half of the seniority list, there will be a lot more captains than first officers. You're still pretty far down there, so it might take awhile."

"Where's the other girl today?" the tailor asked, putting the last pin in my hem and excusing me to change.

"She had to fly," Pam said. "She said she'll be in tomorrow."

"You better sew another stripe on her jacket." I handed him my slacks. "It looks like she's going to be a captain."

∞

"Your letter must have worked." Gene said en route to Bridgeport. "I was down in Providence the other day, and I saw Beth in an upgrade class."

"I don't know if it was my letter or the new vice president," I said, studying the page that depicted the procedure for our approach. It was my leg, and the weather was terrible. It looked like our approach was going to be down to minimums.

"The new vice president made the changes, but it was your letter that inspired him," Gene said. "You might want to add another five knots in case we hit wind shear."

I set my airspeed bug and double-checked my altimeter setting. Gene programmed the approach and missed-approach frequencies into the radios.

"NorCon five-ten, Bridgeport Tower," the controller called.

"Go ahead," Gene said.

"The Citation in front of you reported a ten-knot drop in airspeed half a mile out."

"Roger," Gene said.

I added more power and kept my eyes glued to the airspeed indicator. A change in airspeed would be our first indication of wind shear.

"We don't want to miss this approach," Gene said, studying the radar. It showed a solid red line—the color indicating the most precipitation and therefore the worst weather—across the missed-approach course.

"I'll do my best." It had gotten much darker, and rain began to pound the fuselage. The air was smooth, though, the needles were centered, and the airspeed was holding steady.

But just when I thought everything was under control, it all fell apart. The airspeed decreased ten knots, we fell below the glide slope, and we drifted right of the centerline.

"Add power!" Gene shouted over the sound of the rain.

But I had already given the engines full power. I gingerly brought the nose up, trying to get the airplane to climb without stalling. I turned the control wheel gently to the left, hoping to get back on the centerline. But nothing happened. The airplane kept descending, the airspeed remained too slow, and the centerline stayed to our left.

"I'm showing you *below* the glide slope, NorCon five-ten," the controller called urgently.

"Roger," Gene said.

Gene and I stared at the instruments, willing the airplane to respond. We were both thinking of the power plant with its tall smokestacks that was just to the right of the runway. Several long seconds passed, and then the turbulence hit.

The first jolt slammed us forward against our shoulder harnesses. The next jolt knocked our heads against the ceiling. Then the bumps became a steady assault. I heard the passengers screaming and Gene shouting, but I ignored them as I struggled with the airplane.

Finally, when I thought my arms couldn't possibly hold the control wheel steady for another second, the turbulence stopped. The airspeed began to increase, and I raised the nose until the glide slope needle moved back toward center.

We broke out of the clouds at minimums, right over the runway. I reduced the power and flared. My landing was perfect.

"Nothing like a wet runway for a smooth landing," Gene commented, smiling. "Nice job."

∞

While the airplane was being fueled, Gene and I went into operations to get the updated weather. The cold front that had caused the
bad weather was on its way to Boston, we learned, but we would
probably beat it back.

We each bought a soda and threaded our way through the terminal toward the gate.

"Do you think those two are our pilots?" I heard a man say, as
we waited for the agent to unlock the door to the ramp.

"She's probably a stewardess," his companion said.

I couldn't get rid of this uniform fast enough!

"I hope so. I'm sure as hell not getting on any plane flown by
some chick!"

"I'll second that motion!" Both men laughed.

Gene sauntered over to the two men. "Are you gentlemen going
to Boston?" he asked politely.

"Hopefully," one said.

"I'm Captain Vincent," Gene said, "and that woman is my first
officer." He pointed in my direction.

The men looked embarrassed.

"Did you know she flew the airplane into Bridgeport just now?"
Gene continued. "On final approach we experienced *severe* wind shear.
I wasn't sure we were going to be able to pull out of it, but Kendra
nursed that airplane through and made a textbook-perfect landing.
I couldn't have done it any better myself."

The men stammered something about never having flown with
a woman pilot before.

"Then you can't really judge, can you?" Gene turned and walked
to the door.

"Thanks," I said as we ran through the rain to the airplane.
"You'll probably get in trouble for scaring away two passengers."

"They'll be on the flight," Gene said. "And I want you to fly."

"But it's your leg," I said.

"I'm giving it to you," Gene said, "and we're leaving the cockpit door open. I want those sexist pigs to *see* you fly."

When Beth passed her checkride, Pam and I threw her a surprise party in the pilot lounge. We baked a cake in the shape of an airplane, frosted it in Northeast Connection's colors, and wrote CONGRATU-LATIONS, CAPTAIN BETH! across the fuselage. We picked up her new uniform (with ours) at the tailor's and hung her jacket with its four stripes on the wall. We invited all the Boston-based pilots, the gate agents, the mechanics, the dispatchers, and the baggage handlers, and at least fifty people showed up.

"No one has ever given me a surprise party before," Beth said with tears in her eyes. "I love you all!" She hugged everyone in the room, then put on her jacket and cut the cake.

"How was training?" I asked when I finally got a minute to speak to her alone.

"Really hard," she said. "They expected me to know *everything* in the manual!"

"Were they picky about systems?" I asked. I'd been studying both the systems manual and the pilot's operating handbook in preparation for upgrading.

"More like V-speeds, weights, and limitations," she said.

"That's a relief." I already had the V-speeds, weights, and limitations committed to memory, as was expected of any captain or first officer.

"And the flight training was horrible!" she said, lowering her voice. "My first instructor hated women. Every time I was fifty feet off an altitude or five degrees off a heading, he started yelling that I'd never make captain. I finally went to the head of training and demanded another instructor. So they gave me Brian Young. He's a real sweetie—and totally cute! He said the next time he comes up to Boston he's going to call me for a date—"

"How was the checkride?" I interrupted.

"A nightmare," she said. "The examiner said we were going to keep doing single engine approaches until I got them right, and it took four hours!"

"But you passed," I said. "And that's all that matters."

"I'm a captain now," Beth said, fingering the four stripes on the sleeves of her jacket. "I can't believe it!"

"You look different today," Gene said the next time I flew with him. "Did you change your hair?"

"I'm wearing a new uniform," I said. "Pam, Beth, and I had them made by a tailor in the North End."

"Why?" he asked.

"We couldn't stand wearing polyester," I said.

"What's wrong with polyester?" Gene asked, smiling. "It's washable and it never wrinkles or fades. Just because my wife says the feel of it grates on her like fingernails on a chalkboard . . ."

I laughed. "Do you want the name of the tailor?"

"No, thanks," Gene said. "We had to replace the roof on the house, and now I can't even afford new socks." He slipped his foot out of his shoe to show me the holes in his sock.

"We're not sure the company will approve," I said. "So don't tell anyone."

"Your secret is safe with me."

∞

Pam and I didn't see as much of Beth after she became a captain. She was assigned the most junior captain reserve lines, spending twenty days a month glued to the phone, while we were flying fairly senior first officer lines.

But one day Beth and I were both leaving operations at the same time.

"How's flying as a captain?" I asked. "Is it as great as it's cracked up to be?"

To my surprise, Beth burst into tears.

"What's the matter?" I asked.

She shook her head and ducked into the women's room.

I followed.

"Steve Stiles is an asshole," she cried, sitting down on the couch in the employees-only section.

"Everyone knows that," I said. Steve Stiles was a very unpopular first officer. He'd been hired as a captain, having supposedly flown combat missions in Vietnam, but the new vice president had relegated him to first officer until his seniority warranted otherwise. He was bitter and resentful and took it out on everyone he flew with.

"He told me I was a lousy pilot," Beth sobbed. Her mascara was running down her cheeks, and her blue eye shadow was smeared all around her eyes. "He said I slept my way to the top."

"He's a jerk," I said. "You have to ignore him."

"I didn't sleep my way to the top. I haven't slept with anyone at this company!"

"Of course not," I soothed. "If you had, you would have been a captain much sooner." I laughed, hoping for a smile out of Beth.

"And the worst part is that I got so upset I couldn't fly," she continued without smiling. "I screwed up a landing so bad he had to take over!" She broke into a new fit of sobbing.

"He was harassing and abusing you," I said, putting my arm around her. "Anyone would have trouble concentrating in those circumstances. I think we should call Jenson right now and let him take care of it. I'm sure he knows enough to recognize harassment when he hears about it."

"I can't tell Jenson," she said, walking over to the sink to wash her face.

"Why not?"

"Because if I can't handle a little pressure from a first officer," she said, emptying her purse onto the couch, "he'll think I won't be able to handle an in-flight emergency." She methodically laid out jars, bottles, brushes, and plastic cases on the sink ledge and began to reapply her makeup.

"Harassment has nothing to do with emergencies," I said. "If you let Stiles get away with this, he'll keep harassing you and me and Pam and any other woman pilots he flies with."

"I'm sorry about that," Beth said, concentrating on her image in the mirror. "But you have to understand my feelings. I want you to promise not to tell anyone about this, okay?"

"But Beth . . ." I pleaded, feeling completely frustrated.

"Promise," she said, looking at me. One eye was completely made up, and the other was naked.

"Okay," I said, finally, "I promise."

Jenson, the new vice president, decided to make a marketing event out of Northeast Connection's first all-woman crew. He pulled Beth off reserve and brought Pam in on a scheduled day off. Four seats were booked for journalists, and Beth and Pam's picture made the *Boston Globe,* the airport newsletter, and the company in-flight magazine.

"How was flying with Beth?" I asked Pam the next time I saw her.

"Interesting," she said.

"What does that mean?" I asked. I would have loved to have been part of the company's first all-woman crew.

"You'll understand when you fly with her."

Toward the end of April, when Pam was in upgrade school, I arrived at the airport to find that my captain had called in sick, and Beth was replacing him.

"I've been waiting a long time to be on an all-woman crew," I said, greeting Beth happily. "We're going to have a blast!"

"I know," Beth said. "I love these trips with just the girls. We can gossip, flirt with the controllers, talk girl talk, and not have any pressure from *men!*"

"I'm going to preflight," I said, grabbing my flight bag. "I'll see you out there."

"I'll do it," Beth said. "You can go get set up in the cockpit."

"Really?" I asked. It was the first officer's responsibility to do a preflight walk-around inspection of the aircraft before every takeoff. The preflight was considered a necessary but onerous chore which no self-respecting captain would be caught dead performing—unless the captain didn't trust the first officer.

"It's not that I don't trust you," Beth said. "It's just that being a new captain—well, you know how it is. I like to make sure of things myself."

∞

Beth flew the first leg of our trip from Boston to New Haven. It was the captain's privilege to choose which segments she flew, and most captains chose to fly the first leg, alternating with the first officer for the rest of the trip.

But Beth flew the second leg from New Haven to New York, as well.

"I get a little nervous flying into La Guardia," she said. "I feel more comfortable doing it myself. You can fly the next two legs, okay?"

"Okay," I said, agreeably. I didn't especially care which airports I flew into.

When Beth taxied all the way onto the runway for takeoff at La Guardia, I thought she'd changed her mind about letting me fly. And when she pushed the power levers forward, I resigned myself to working the radios for another leg. So when the tower cleared us for takeoff and Beth signaled for me to take the controls, I was surprised.

"What's going on?" I asked.

"It's your leg," Beth said. "I told you that before."

"NorCon five-fourteen, cleared for *immediate* takeoff," the controller repeated.

"Hurry up," Beth said nervously.

I quickly moved my seat forward enough to reach the rudder pedals and continued the takeoff. When we reached cruising altitude I apologized to Beth for not being ready, explaining how I'd wrongly assumed that by taxiing to the runway herself she was going to fly again.

"You shouldn't make assumptions," she said huffily. "Every captain does things differently."

"Now that I know how you do things, I'll be prepared." I'd flown with at least twenty different captains at Northeast Connection, and every one of them had let me taxi, but I didn't want to spoil our trip by arguing with Beth.

"NorCon five-fourteen, report Bradley in sight for a visual," the controller called.

"I haven't even gotten the weather or called operations or anything!" Beth shrieked.

"We're still thirty miles out." I pointed to our distance measuring equipment, which was set to the airport frequency.

But Beth was already listening to the recorded weather information and didn't respond. "Here," she said, handing me a crumpled piece of paper and tuning her radio to Northeast Connection's company frequency at Bradley, where she announced us ten minutes out.

I looked over the weather. The airport was reporting three miles visibility in haze, and they were using runway six. Runway six meant a straight-in approach from our direction, and judging from the murk we were flying through, we weren't going to see the airport in time for a visual approach.

"I think we should ask for the ILS," I suggested.

"He wants us to do a visual," she said.

"But we're not going to see it—"

"You fly," Beth said. "I'll look."

"Let me know when you've got the airport," the controller said.

"Roger," Beth replied.

I flew the airplane.

"I think I've got it," Beth said.

I squinted through the windshield. We were still fifteen miles away, so if Beth was actually seeing the airport she had amazing eyesight.

"NorCon five-fourteen has the airport in sight," Beth told the controller.

"NorCon five-fourteen, cleared for a visual approach, runway six, Bradley International," the controller said.

"Turn right about thirty degrees," Beth said.

"Why?" Even though we were doing a visual approach, I had put the ILS frequency in my navigation radio for guidance.

"The airport is off to the right," she said.

"No, it's not. Look at the needle." The needle showed us on the extended centerline of the runway.

"It's probably unreliable," Beth said. "Didn't we read something about them working on the ILS today?"

"I don't remember anything like that," I answered.

"That's why the controller wanted us to do a visual," Beth said, grabbing the controls. "I told you to turn right! Now we're going to miss the airport." She cranked the controls to the right.

"Jesus, Beth!" I cried. "What are you doing?"

"Bradley Approach, NorCon five-fourteen," she called on the radio. "We're a little high for a straight-in. Is it okay if we fly overhead and do a left downwind?"

"Cleared as requested," the controller said. Beth still had the controls, and she put us in a steep descent.

"We're still ten miles south," I said. "There's the river." I pointed out the windshield. "Bradley is on the *other* side of the river!" I marked a big *X* on the map and tried to show Beth where we were, but she wouldn't look.

"I'm the captain here," she said. "Don't tell me what to do!"

"NorCon five-fourteen, say intentions," the controller said.

"Visual approach for runway six," Beth said.

"I show you in the traffic pattern over Rentschler Airport. Turn left to a heading of three-three-zero and maintain three thousand," the controller said.

"Turning to three-three-zero," Beth responded, handing me back the controls.

I took them without comment.

"I can't believe that controller thought we were going to land at the wrong airport!" Beth said. "He's acting like we didn't know where we were going! I bet it's because we're women. He wouldn't treat men like that."

I concentrated on the approach and landing while Beth worked the radios. She was calmer than she'd been all day, which didn't make sense because she, as captain, could lose her license over this.

When Beth didn't take the controls after landing, I taxied us to the gate. While we were taxiing, the controller gave us the radar room's phone number and asked us to call ASAP.

"I'll go call," Beth said, shutting down the engines. "You can do the walk-around and load the passengers."

I inspected the airplane, wondering if this incident was going to jeopardize my chances of upgrading to captain. It was a selfish thought, but it wasn't my fault Beth hadn't listened to me.

She came back grinning.

"What happened?" I asked.

"I just explained that I had a new copilot who got a little confused in the haze—"

"You what?" I interrupted.

"Relax, Kendra," Beth said, fastening her seat belt. "He didn't ask for any names. No one will know it was you. I charmed the guy. He said he'd trained a lot of new controllers and he knew what it was like keeping his mouth shut and letting them make mistakes. He even invited me up there to meet him the next time I'm here."

"But Beth," I said, trying to control my temper. "I'm *not* a new copilot, and I'm *not* the one who put us over the wrong airport—"

"All's well that ends well, okay?" she said, starting the engines. "The controller didn't want to make a big deal out of it. I don't want to make a big deal out of it. And I'm sure you don't want to make a big deal out of it either."

I fumed silently.

"It's your leg," she said. "If you're comfortable taxiing yourself, go ahead."

"Have you flown with Beth yet?" Gene asked between Boston and Burlington.

"Once," I said.

"How was it?"

"Okay," I answered.

"Okay?" Gene looked at me and raised his eyebrows.

I felt disloyal saying something negative about another woman, but I was so upset I told him the whole story.

"I'm not surprised," he said. "She was like that as a first officer."

"I thought that because we were both women it would be wonderful flying together," I said. "You know, we'd have some sort of bond—"

"It doesn't always work that way," Gene said.

"So I learned."

"You were right about the discrimination," Pam said, unwrapping a package of Hostess cupcakes. We were sitting outside on an empty baggage cart eating our lunch. "They made Beth the token woman captain, and they're blowing off the rest of us." Pam's ground school class had been canceled after the first week when Jenson decided Northeast Connection already had too many captains.

"I could write another letter," I said. "If both of us signed it, they might get nervous."

"I don't know," Pam said, dipping a cupcake into a carton of milk. "If only a major airline would hire me, I could just leave and not worry about it."

The door to operations banged open, and Beth came running across the ramp. "Guess what!" she called, waving a piece of paper. "You won't believe it!"

"What?" we chorused.

"I got hired by United!" she shouted, hugging each of us.

"I didn't know you'd had an interview," Pam said dryly.

"Congratulations," I added without enthusiasm. Beth and I had never talked about our trip together, and I was still angry.

"I didn't want to tell anyone until I found out for sure," Beth gushed. "My dad had a pretty good idea, because one of his ALPA friends put in a good word, but he told me not to tell anyone until I saw it in writing. When I got the letter I had to drive down here to show you girls right away."

"When do you start?" I asked.

"Not for a month," she said. "I thought about taking a vacation for a couple weeks, but I'd rather keep flying. I might as well log captain time while I can. It's going to be a few years before I sit in the left seat again."

"Just because you have a job with a major airline is no reason to give up your seat," Pam said sarcastically. "It's not as if anyone around here would like the chance to be a captain."

"What do you mean?" Beth seemed surprised that we weren't as excited about her new job as she was.

"If you can't figure it out, I don't know how you're going to make it through ground school," Pam said, carrying her cupcake wrapper and milk carton to the trash, then opening the door to operations.

"What's the matter with her?" Beth asked me.

"They canceled her upgrade class," I said, stuffing my garbage into my lunch bag.

"So?" Beth asked.

"She's disappointed," I said, standing up and brushing crumbs off my slacks.

"As soon as there's a slot they'll finish training her," Beth said.

"That's the point," I said, picking up my flight bag. "You have another job to go to, yet you're holding on to your captain seat here."

"But it's my seat," Beth said. "I don't have to give it up just because Pam's class was canceled. It's not my fault!"

"You asked what was wrong with Pam," I said, walking toward my airplane. "And I told you. I'm not going to stand here and argue about it."

"You're just jealous!" Beth shouted across the ramp.

"You're right!" I shouted back, leaving my flight bag at the foot of the steps. I performed the preflight by rote, not really seeing anything I checked. When I finished, I looked back toward the terminal and saw Beth sitting alone on the baggage cart, cradling her letter.

SIMULATION

Given the fact that the ratio of men to women in commercial aviation was a hundred to one, it didn't come as a huge surprise to find myself the only woman in the new-hire 727 class at Hemisphere Airlines in Houston. My mother was full of foreboding. Did I know about the research establishing that girls and women learn better in all-female groups? Was I aware of the phenomenon of tokenism and its implications in an educational environment? She didn't want to alarm me, but, considering the data, she didn't see how I would be able to master enough material in such unfavorable circumstances to responsibly pilot an eighty-five-ton airplane with a hundred and fifty trusting passengers.

It wasn't going to be easy, I discovered.

"I don't care if y'all were flying fighter jets in the Persian Gulf or towing banners over Daytona Beach," Chuck Powalsky, the instructor, roared in greeting on the first morning of ground school. "From now on, y'all are going to be *second officers*. Flight engineers! Third-in-commands! Sideways-seaters! The lowliest scum in the pilot pool!" He drank from a carton of chocolate milk he'd carried with him into the classroom, pausing to gauge our reaction. The sixteen men and I slunk low in our chairs.

"He's acting tough to compensate for his height," the man sitting next to me wrote on a piece of notebook paper and pushed in my direction. Chuck Powalsky was short, five feet four at the most. And that was in cowboy boots with three-inch heels.

"That is, if y'all even manage to *pass* my ground school," Chuck continued. "The washout rate is ten percent. That means one point seven of you are going to be looking for new jobs within the month!"

"Short people always think they have to prove something," my neighbor wrote.

"I'm short," I wrote back.

"You're petite," he wrote, smiling at me. He had sparkling hazel eyes, very white teeth, and full red lips. Kissable lips.

"I see we have a la-dy in here!" Chuck bellowed, seeming to notice me for the first time. "The washout rate for la-dies is thirty percent."

While we were waiting in line to have our ID pictures taken, my seatmate introduced himself as Brett from Cleveland, currently residing at the Airport Inn (where Hemisphere was housing us during training), room 207.

"Have you heard how they plan to establish seniority within our class?" he asked.

"No," I said. But I was curious. Seniority governed base and airplane assignments, upgrade time, monthly schedules, vacations, and pay. Hemisphere had crew bases in Houston, Cleveland, Newark, Seattle, and Guam (they'd gotten the Guam routes and base when they'd acquired Micronesian Airways ten years before). I was happy in the Victorian house I shared with Karen and three other women in Cambridge, and I enjoyed taking classes at the Harvard Extension, playing tennis at the Mount Auburn Club, and volunteering at the Women's Center. I had no desire to move. Since Hemisphere had flights every hour between Newark and Boston, it would be a relatively easy commute.

"First I heard they were going to use the last four digits of our Social Security numbers—with the lowest number being the most senior," Brett said. "That would have been great for me because mine begins with one. But then I heard they were going to use our grade point averages—"

"Grade point averages?" I asked.

"Scores from our ground school tests, simulator sessions, and even the final checkride."

"I guess that's as fair as anything," I said. Especially since the last four digits of my Social Security number began with seven.

"There are only two openings for second officers in Cleveland," Brett said, "so I have to make sure I wind up senior enough to get one of them."

"Seven-two-seven ground school is going to be the hardest class y'all have ever taken," Chuck said, passing out airplane and company operations manuals. "Y'all may think it's the material that makes it so hard, or y'all may think it's me. But your real enemy here is *time*."

I flipped through the 727 manual. It was filled with complex systems diagrams. I was not a systems person.

"This company," Chuck continued, "expects me to make second officers out of y'all in one short month. Even if you breathe, eat, shit, and dream of the Boeing Seven-Two-Seven, y'all won't have enough *time* to learn everything you need to know." He began distributing workbooks and handouts. "Tests are Monday, Wednesday, and Friday mornings. I suggest y'all organize yourselves into study groups. This ain't the kind of material you can learn by yourselves."

"Do you want to study together?" Brett wrote.

"Sure," I wrote back.

Tuesday and Thursday afternoons were reserved for simulator training. We were divided into groups of four or five and assigned a two-hour block in the simulator. My group consisted of Brett, myself, and two men named Sherman and Ed.

"I've been thinking about volunteering for Guam," Sherman said while we were sitting in the simulator building lobby, waiting to meet our instructor. Sherman, at forty-four, was the oldest in the class. He'd flown for an airline that had gone out of business fifteen years ago and had been selling cars since.

"I hear you only fly ten days a month out there," Ed said, spitting a wad of tobacco into a can he carried around with him. Ed was from Montana and had flown as a crop duster pilot before coming to Hemisphere.

"And you're guaranteed two consecutive weeks off a month," Sherman said, stubbing out one cigarette and lighting another. "I figure I can leave the wife in Denver and get a crash pad in Guam. That way I can have a little fun with those Asian beauties for half the month and be at home for the other half."

I wanted to ask Sherman what his wife thought of his plan.

"I'm thinking of doing the same in about six months," Brett said.

"I have some business to tie up in Cleveland, and then I'm a free agent."

"Where do you want to be based, Kendra?" Sherman asked.

"Newark," I said.

"*Sewer*-k?" Sherman looked at me in disbelief. "Why would you want to go there?"

"I live in Boston," I said. "Newark is the closest base."

"It's all yours," Sherman said.

The simulator instructor was a soft-spoken pilot named Al, who had left the line for the training department because he wanted more nights at home. We followed him through a maze of catwalks to the 727 simulator, which was essentially a cockpit on long hydraulic legs. The hydraulics enabled it to move on all three axes, simulating an airplane in actual flight.

"Today I'll walk you through the cockpit and panel preflight checks," Al said in his very quiet voice, leading us into the simulator. It was identical to a 727 cockpit with forward-facing seats for the captain and first officer, a jump seat behind the captain, and the second officer's "sideways" seat behind the first officer. The second officer sat at a desk (used for paperwork such as weight and balance) facing a panel of switches, gauges, and lights for which she or he was responsible. "By Thursday all of this should be memorized."

Brett and I had agreed to organize and read the material on our own and get together to study for the first test in his room at nine. Although I'd been studying since dinner, I'd also taken a shower and put on a fresh T-shirt and shorts.

"The air-conditioning isn't working in here," he said when I arrived with my books. He was wearing a pair of running shorts without a shirt, and I could see he had a very, very nice body.

"Do you want to use my room?" I asked.

"That's okay," he said. "I ran into the guys at happy hour and invited them to join us." I looked into the room and saw, to my great disappointment, Sherman and Ed. Sherman had appropriated the only chair, where he was smoking and drinking beer, his gut hanging over the waistband of his plaid Bermudas. Ed was sprawled on Brett's bed with a beer in one hand and his spitting can in the other. His back, I observed, was covered with acne, and his shorts looked suspiciously like boxers. Brett's book and papers were spread out on the inoperative air conditioner.

"What are we studying?" I asked, sitting down on the floor and trying to overcome the fact that in order to be part of a study group I was trapped in a hot and smoky hotel room with three men, one of whom appeared to be in just his underwear.

"Airplane dimensions and limitations," Sherman said, exhaling a cloud of smoke. The subject for the test was "Airplane: General." "What's the wingspan of a -200?" Since the company flew both 727-100s and 727-200s, we were required to know the systems of both.

"I have no idea," I said, coughing and fanning myself with my notebook. Because the room was supposed to be climate-controlled, the windows didn't open.

"If you're hot you can take off your shirt," Ed suggested, spewing a long, brown stream into his can.

"I'm not *that* hot," I said, feeling queasy.

"A hundred and eight feet," Brett responded to Sherman's question, twisting the cap off a bottle of beer. "How about the height of the tail off the ground?"

"Thirty-four feet," Sherman answered. "Can you hand me

another?" Brett passed Sherman a beer from his minibar refrigerator. I noticed there were already eight empty beer bottles lined up on the top.

"I got the impression it was more important to learn about the emergency equipment," I said. Not only was my evening with Brett ruined, and not only was my "study group" inebriated, but they weren't even studying the right material.

"Don't waste your time," Sherman said. "Emergency equipment only counts for ten percent of the test."

"How do you know?"

"Trust us, Kendra," Brett said, winking at me. "We have good intuition."

"I hope y'all didn't stay up too late studying," Chuck said, cheerfully passing out the tests the next morning. "This is one of my easier exams." He laughed.

"Sadistic bastard," Brett wrote.

I nodded in agreement. We'd studied in Brett's room until after midnight, and then I'd set my alarm for six A.M. to go over the areas we hadn't covered.

"Y'all heard the one about how the flight is almost over, and the first officer makes the announcement that the skies are clear, the temperature is sixty-five, and they'll be on the ground shortly?"

No one answered, and Chuck continued.

"But the first officer forgets to turn off the PA. Suddenly the captain's voice comes over the speakers in the cabin saying, 'If I only had a cup of coffee and a blow job, the day would be complete.' The first flight attendant goes running up to the cockpit to tell the captain that the PA is still on. As she runs through first class, one of the passengers stops her and says, 'Hey, you forgot the coffee.' "

"I've only heard that one about a million times," Brett wrote, laughing with the rest of the class.

I was too tired to laugh.

"Y'all get an hour to take this exam," Chuck said, still chuckling at his joke. "Eighty percent or above is passing. The first one you fail is a freebie. The second means you're heading home on a one-way pass."

I read through the multiple-choice questions and tried not to panic. I hadn't studied the right material, I realized. The test was composed of trivia and details, and I'd spent my time learning general concepts. I looked around the room to see how the rest of the class was faring, but they were eagerly filling in the circles on their answer sheets. Chuck was standing in the doorway drinking his chocolate milk, staring at me over the top of the carton. His lank brown hair was hanging down over his forehead, and his eyes looked small and dark. I couldn't help but notice his resemblance to a vulture, and I had to pinch myself to keep from nervously laughing.

Of course, there wouldn't be much to laugh about if I failed the test, so I started with the questions I knew. The wingspan of the -200? One hundred eight sounded familiar. And the height of the tail off the ground? Thirty-four rang a bell. Or was it forty-three? I remembered hearing that it's better to go with the first answer that crosses your mind. I circled thirty-four. Minimum pressure of the oxygen bottles? Fifteen hundred. Minimum pressure of the escape slides? I left that blank. Number of emergency exits on a -100? Maximum zero-fuel weight of a -200?

I did the best I could, surprised at the number of answers that jumped out at me from the study session.

∞

"How'd you do on the test?" Brett asked. During the simulator sessions, we rotated seats so that everyone got half an hour at the second officer panel, in each of the pilot seats, and on the jump seat. Ed was in the jump seat, and Brett and I were in the pilot seats watching Sherman struggle with his preflight flow pattern on the panel. He hadn't memorized it before the lesson, and now he was trying to bluff his way through.

"Eighty-eight," I said, overjoyed that I had done so well.

"I got a ninety-six," Brett said. "I missed the one about the escape-slide pressures. I couldn't remember if it was twenty-seven hundred or three thousand."

"I missed that one, too," I said.

"We forgot to go over it," Brett said. "Tonight we'll be more thorough."

Having scored a ninety-two on the second test, I didn't question Sherman or Brett when they said the third test would probably empha-size the auxiliary power unit start sequence. I listened carefully and took notes as we went over the questions in the workbook, quizzed one another on the limitations, and each recited the start sequence. By ten-thirty we'd covered all the material.

"Want to go for a walk to the 7-Eleven?" Brett asked as we were gathering our books and papers.

I was exhausted from staying up late every night to study either for a simulator session or a test, but the 7-Eleven was only a few blocks away, and I didn't want to pass up a chance to be together with Brett. "Okay."

"The guys never leave us any time alone," he said, reaching for my hand as we crossed under the highway that ran alongside the hotel.

"Maybe the two of us could study by ourselves from now on," I said, feeling tingles of pleasure radiate up my arm.

"I wish we could," he said, releasing my hand to open the door of the 7-Eleven. "But it's been helpful having them around. Look how well we've been doing on the tests."

"We could do just as well without them," I said, carrying a carton of juice, a bunch of bananas, and a box of Pop-Tarts to the register. I'd discovered it was faster (and cheaper) to eat breakfast in my room than to go to the hotel's restaurant.

"No, we couldn't," Brett said, paying for two jars of peanuts and a six-pack of beer. "You see, the guys seem to have a *feel* for what's going to be on the tests." He held the door open, and we started back to the Airport Inn.

"A *feel?*"

"Put it this way," he said, lowering his voice, even though we were alone on the sidewalk. "We could maybe lose Sherman, but we need Ed."

"Ed? All he does is spit."

Brett laughed. "He contributes more than anyone else," he said, leaning against a car. We were in the hotel parking lot, and it was dark. "How do you think we always know what's going to be on the tests?"

"From Ed?" I asked, incredulous.

"Ed has a friend," Brett said, putting his bag down on the ground and taking my bag out of my arms. We were standing very close together. "His friend was in Chuck's ground school last month. For the right price, his friend has a very good memory."

"You mean he pays his friend money to tell him what's on the tests?" I asked.

Brett pulled me close and ran his hands though my hair. I felt myself melting against him.

"Isn't that cheating?" I asked, inhaling the clean cotton smell of his T-shirt.

"How is it cheating?" he countered. "Do we have copies of the tests? Do we look at other people's answers in class? Do we write notes on our palms?" He bent down to kiss me. "I've been wanting to do that since I first saw you." He kissed me again. His lips were as good as they'd looked.

"I wish we had more time," he said, reluctantly releasing me, picking up our two bags, and handing me mine.

"Me, too," I said.

When we parted at the elevator, Brett checked the hall in both directions before giving me a brief kiss. "I'll be dreaming about you," he whispered.

The morning after the third test there were only sixteen people in the class.

"That's one gone, point seven to go," Chuck said, gesturing to the empty seat. "Y'all need to be studying this material in groups. Forrest thought he could do it himself."

Everyone looked at Dave Forrest's empty chair.

"So," Chuck said, "what's the best way to get an ugly flight attendant to suck your dick?" He took a sip of chocolate milk.

No one volunteered an answer.

"Dip it in Alpo first!"

The class laughed. I attempted a smile, but I don't think I pulled it off because Chuck glared at me.

"Do you notice a theme to Chuck's jokes?" Brett wrote.

"Immaturity," I wrote back.

"My guess is sexual frustration," Brett wrote. "Can you imagine who in her right mind would want to spend any time with him?"

∞

"Let's get rid of Sherman and Ed early tonight," Brett said as we were walking back from lunch in the airport employee cafeteria where, with our new Hemisphere IDs, we got a hefty discount.

"Our study session isn't until eight," I said. "We could take a picnic into the park." There was a public park with several miles of wooded trails behind the hotel. I jogged there every afternoon. It was quiet, peaceful, and potentially romantic.

"Better make it after studying," Brett said. "I don't want to miss happy hour. For the price of a beer I can fill up on free food and not have to worry about dinner."

"I'll come to happy hour with you," I offered. "Then we can go for a walk."

"It gets pretty rowdy."

"The Terminal gets rowdy?" I asked. The Terminal was the hotel's bar. It had model airplanes hanging from the ceiling and airplane seats at the tables. Although it boasted a happy hour with the best Cajun shrimp in Houston and attracted a lot of airline people, The Terminal was not exactly rowdy.

"We don't always go to The Terminal," Brett said. "Sometimes we try other bars in the area."

"How do you get there?" The only place within walking distance of the hotel was the 7-Eleven, and none of us had cars.

"Chuck takes us in his truck."

"Chuck?" I asked. "Our instructor?"

"The one and only."

"I'm not sure I understand this," I said, not understanding at all. "You go to bars with Chuck?"

"The bars are pretty slimy," Brett said. "But Chuck gets real talkative after he's had a few drinks, and sometimes he talks about the tests. It can't hurt to be friendly with the guy who controls your career. Besides, we always share everything we find out with you at the study sessions."

"I could still go with you."

"I told you, Kendra, these bars are not like The Terminal. Some of them have topless waitresses and other stuff. Anyway, I have a better idea," he said, changing the subject. "How about if I sneak into your room tonight?"

Brett was furious. Al had let us see our training folders, which listed the maneuvers we'd performed each period and the grades he'd assigned. The grades were on a scale of one to five, with one being excellent and five being failure. Three was average. "Did he give all of us straight threes, or is he just punishing me?" he asked as we walked from the simulator building back to the hotel.

"I got all threes," I said.

"Me, too," Sherman said, lighting a cigarette.

"Same here," Ed said, spitting on the sidewalk.

"That pisses me off," Brett fumed. "We're leading the class in test scores, but these simulator grades are going to put us back in the middle of the pack somewhere."

"We should demand another instructor," Sherman said.

"I heard that Al is one of the easiest," Ed said.

"How easy can he be if he's giving us such lousy grades?" Sherman asked.

"He's giving us all the *same* lousy grades," I said. "So it doesn't really matter—"

"Look, Kendra," Sherman interrupted. "*We* need to come out of this class with decent seniority numbers. We have more responsibilities than you do. Ed has a mortgage on his ranch. And Brett and I have families to support—"

"Families?" I asked, looking directly at Brett. "What kind of family?"

"I'm in the process of getting divorced—"

"You're married?" I stopped in the middle of the sidewalk. Brett and I had been spending almost every evening together, and he had never mentioned anything about being married! "Why didn't you tell me?"

"You never asked," he replied, walking back to me and motioning Sherman and Ed to continue to the hotel. "Anyway, they have nothing to do with us."

"*They?*" I practically shouted. "You mean there are kids, too?"

"Brett Junior is eight, and Katie is six. They live with their mother."

"I can't believe you kept this a secret from me!"

"It wasn't a secret," he said, trying to put his arms around me. "I would have told you if you'd asked. I didn't want to bring it up because it's painful for me to be reminded that my marriage failed and she got the kids."

"But I guess it wasn't too painful to tell Sherman and Ed," I said, moving out of his reach.

"That's different. They're men. They can identify with me."

"You are so full of shit!" I fumed. "I was such an idiot to ever trust you!" I turned and ran down the sidewalk.

"Wait," Brett called, running after me. "We haven't finished our conversation."

"Leave me alone," I said, jogging toward the hotel. "I have to study."

"You can't study by yourself," he said, catching up and grabbing my arm. "You'll never pass the test."

"I passed yesterday." I shook off his hand.

"Barely. And only because I told you what to study."

"Well, I don't need you telling me anything from now on!" We had reached the hotel, and I raced through the lobby and up the fire stairs so no one in the elevator would see me cry.

In the morning my eyes were red and swollen from lack of sleep. I'd studied the pneumatic system until one in the morning, then gotten up at five to reread my notes. The chapter was long and complicated, and I wasn't brimming with confidence as I entered the classroom.

"Hi, Kendra," Brett said, as if nothing were wrong.

I walked past him and sat down at a desk in the back corner of the room.

"Why are you wearing sunglasses?" he asked, following me to my new seat. He tried to remove them.

I shoved his hand out of the way.

"I'm getting some coffee," Sherman said, standing in front of my desk. "Can I bring you a cup?"

"No, thank you," I said, opening my book.

"Morning," Ed said, joining Brett and Sherman. He spit into his can.

"I'm trying to study," I said.

"We made an effort," I heard Sherman say as the three of them walked away. "If that's the way she wants it . . ."

I knew I'd failed the test as soon as Chuck passed it out. Half the questions were taken from the pneumatic system of the 727-100, and I'd forgotten to read the section describing differences between the two models. I answered the questions relating to the -200 and guessed on the others.

"What's the captain's favorite kind of birth control?" Chuck asked, as he collected the answer sheets. "The sponge. Because after sex, the flight attendant can use it to wash the dishes."

Everyone laughed except me.

"Kendra doesn't get it," Chuck said. "Can someone explain it to her?"

"I get it," I said. "I just don't think it's funny."

"She's having a bad day," Brett said.

"It must be PMS," Sherman said. "It turns otherwise nice women into bitches."

If they said one more thing, I was leaving.

"That reminds me," Chuck said. "Did you hear about the flight attendant with PMS?"

I got up and walked out, their laughter ringing in my ears.

"Do you have a problem with the way I conduct my class?" Chuck asked when I came out of the women's room, where I'd spent the rest of the morning locked in one of the stalls.

I tried to go back inside, but Chuck barricaded the door.

"There's no point in hiding from me," he said. "If you want to fly for this airline, you have to complete my ground school. If something's bothering you, we might as well get it out in the open."

"Your jokes are insulting," I said.

"Insulting to who?" Chuck asked. "Pilots? You're all pilots. Flight attendants? All pilots joke about flight attendants."

"They make me uncomfortable," I said, standing up straighter.

If Chuck hadn't been wearing his high-heeled boots, I would have been taller than him.

"Then maybe you should rethink your career," Chuck said. "Because you're going to be hearing a lot more jokes in the cockpit, and if you can't take it now, it's only going to get worse."

I remained silent.

"You know what I think your problem is?" he continued, stepping so close I could smell his sour-milk breath. "You and your boyfriend had a little spat, and you're blaming me because I'm a man."

"That's ridiculous!" I yelled, backing away.

"Is it?" he asked, with a mean little grin.

After lunch, Chuck passed back our tests. When he got to mine, he looked at it and shook his head. "I see we may have found our point seven," he said.

My score was a seventy-nine.

"We'd like to talk to you about our simulator grades," Brett told Al when we reported for our next simulator session.

"Okay," Al said. "What seems to be the problem?"

"You gave all of us threes on every maneuver," Sherman said.

"That's true," Al agreed.

"We think we deserve better than that," Brett said. "A three is average. We've been devoting extra time and effort to being above average. We don't understand why you're punishing us."

"I'm not punishing you," Al said, looking confused. "Those grades don't count for anything. We use threes like check marks to show that we've covered a maneuver. All the instructors do it that way."

"How about using ones, then?" Brett suggested.

"Is that what you all want?"

Brett, Sherman, and Ed nodded. I stayed out of it.

"Okay, then," Al said. "Whose day is it to go first?"

I started studying the hydraulic system as soon as I got back to the room. I would study all night if I had to, but I was not going to let Chuck wash me out of ground school.

At ten the phone rang.

"Can I come over?" Brett asked.

"Drop dead," I said.

"Come on, Kendra. We had a lot going for us. You don't want to give up all that because of a little misunderstanding."

I hung up the phone.

Half an hour later it rang again.

"Make sure you know everything about the pumps," Brett said.

"I guess you passed the test," Brett said during our next simulator session. I was taking my turn in the second officer's seat, and he was in the jump seat behind me. Sherman and Ed were in the two pilot seats, and Al was at the control panel programming the scenario we were going to fly. "Otherwise you wouldn't be here."

I stared at the panel.

"She's got PMS again," Sherman said.

"Everyone ready?" Al asked, turning his chair around so he could see the panel.

We all nodded.

"We're climbing out of twenty-five thousand for thirty-three thousand feet," Al said. "Deal with any problems as a crew and pretend I'm not here." He pushed a button, and the simulator began to move.

It was obvious that something was going to go wrong, and I

repeatedly scanned the gauges, dials, and lights on the panel hoping to catch whatever it was.

"Engine failure," Sherman called from the left seat.

I raced into action. In the case of an engine failure, the second officer had three things to do immediately—protect essential power by moving the essential power selector switch to an operating generator; download the remaining generators by removing power from certain high-draw electric systems; and cover the bus by making sure all the bus-tie breakers were connected to the bus-tie bar in order to maximize the working systems.

I completed my three tasks just as Sherman called for the Engine Failure/Fire checklist.

All the required checklists were usually kept in the first officer's seat pocket, which was directly in front of the second officer. I knew the checklists were onboard before departure. I had seen them during my thorough preflight inspection. But, for some reason, I couldn't find the emergency checklist among the others.

"Any year now," Sherman called.

I suddenly remembered where it was. I'd removed some weight and balance forms from the seat pocket and stowed them in the desk. I must have picked up the emergency checklist by mistake. I tried to open the desk, but Ed's seat was so far back it wouldn't open.

"Could you please move your seat forward so I can open the desk?" I asked.

"That's the thing about women," Brett commented. "They only speak when they want something."

Ed moved his seat forward a tiny bit, but it wasn't enough.

"Could you move it a little more, please?"

"If I move any farther my legs will be uncomfortable," Ed said, spitting into his can. It landed with a gurgle and plop.

"What's the emergency checklist doing in the desk, anyway?" Sherman asked. "Isn't it supposed to be kept in the seat pocket?"

"If Ed would just move his seat . . ." I said.

Sherman and Ed looked at each other and rolled their eyes. Ed finally moved his seat, I removed the checklist from the desk, and we finished the procedure. Al gave Sherman, Ed, and me fives for the lesson. Brett got a three because he'd been in the jump seat and not a part of the crew at the time.

The ground school final exam was scheduled for the last Monday of class. I studied Friday night and all day Saturday, taking only short breaks to eat and shower.

I might not have seen another person all weekend, except that on Saturday night I ran into one of the guys from class at the ice machine. His name was Tim, and he sat on the other side of the room.

"Been studying hard?" he asked.

"This is the first time I've left my room," I said.

"Me, too," he said.

Tim filled his ice bucket and moved out of the way so I could fill mine.

"I was wondering," he began shyly, "I mean, I noticed that you don't sit with that group anymore, and I was wondering if you had anyone to study with. A bunch of us are getting together tomorrow at noon, and you'd be welcome to join us."

"Thanks," I said, smiling for the first time in a week. "That would be great."

The next day I met Tim and five other men from class in one of the hotel's conference rooms.

"How come that clique of yours always knows what's going to be on the tests?" one of the men asked. His name was Bob and he was built like a football player.

"I'm not in a clique," I said.

"Anymore," Bob said.

Tim glanced at me apologetically.

"Are they getting the questions from someone who already took the class?" Bob continued. "Or are they getting the tests from someone in the training department?"

"I don't know," I said.

"Put it this way," Bob said. "If we each contributed say, twenty bucks, do you think they'd share their information?"

"You'd have to ask them yourself," I said. This was not what I had in mind in terms of studying. The final was in less than twenty hours, and I had a lot more to learn.

"What room do they meet in?" Bob asked.

I gave them Brett's room number.

"I'll be back," Bob said, heading out the door.

"Might as well get started," Tim said, opening up a yellow booklet with the Hemisphere logo on the cover. I had never seen the booklet before, and I wondered where he'd gotten it. "I'll just ask random questions, okay?"

Everyone nodded.

"Identify the functions of the three sensors on the discharge side of the air-conditioning pack compressor . . ."

Bob came back and reported that no one was in the room, and he couldn't find Brett, Ed, or Sherman anywhere else in the hotel.

The group continued to ask one another questions for two hours. They were good questions, a few of which I recognized from the tests we had already taken.

"Where did you get that book with the questions?" I asked Tim during a break.

"We paid fifty bucks to this guy who was switching to the MD-80. He said he bought it from some captain back when he was on the 727."

"Good morning, y'all," Chuck said. "Everyone ready for my magnum opus?"

There were groans. Chuck took a drink of his chocolate milk.

"I've got a good one for you. What's the definition of an eleven?"

I saw Brett write a note to Sherman.

"A ten who swallows!" Chuck roared, slapping his knees.

Pass or fail, I told myself, after today I'll never have to see Chuck again.

"You've got four hours," he said, handing out the thick pamphlets that comprised the final exam. "Scores will be posted outside the ground school office at three o'clock. Good luck."

"I wasn't sure we'd see you here," Brett said at our last simulator session. "That final was pretty grueling. If we hadn't had our study group, we probably all would have failed."

It was my turn to go first, and I took my place at the panel.

"She probably bribed Chuck," Sherman said from the jump seat. "Told him she was an eleven."

"He must have dipped it in Alpo first," Ed contributed, spitting into his can.

All the lights in the simulator suddenly went out.

"What I want to know is if she used a sponge," Sherman said.

It looks like a loss of all generators, I told myself. The first thing to do is switch essential power to standby. Then, check to make sure the battery switch is on. Next, close the generator field relays. Open all the fuel cross feeds. And there was one more thing I was supposed to have memorized. What was it?

"And if she did, did she do the dishes afterward?" Sherman continued.

"You forgot something," Al told me.

What was that last thing? I absolutely couldn't remember.

"Loss of all generators is on every checkride, and the first five actions have to be performed from memory," Al said.

"I know," I said. "I had them memorized."

"What happened?" Al asked.

"I guess we distracted her," Ed said.

"Hell, if she can't take a little pressure, she shouldn't be a pilot," Sherman said.

"Gentlemen, please," Al pleaded softly. "We have a lot to cover today."

I picked up the checklist to continue the procedure for loss of all generators, but I found there wasn't enough light to read it. Then I remembered the fifth action: Dome lights on.

The checkride that would give us our FAA flight engineer ratings had two parts: an oral exam with one of the airline's FAA-designated examiners, and a simulator ride with a company check airman.

I reported to my oral on Thursday. There had been so much to study I hadn't gotten more than a few hours of sleep or eaten a real meal in three days. I had reread the entire airplane manual, memorized the answers to every workbook question, and studied normal, abnormal, and emergency procedures until I couldn't see straight.

"I'm Dan Carruthers," the examiner said, holding out his hand. He was dressed in a tennis warm-up suit. "I apologize for the outfit, but I'm in the finals of the company tournament at five, and it's always hard to tell how long these orals will take."

Dan Carruthers, I recalled, was the head of all 727 ground training. Chuck had referred to him as the hardest examiner in the department.

"Have a seat," Dan said, leading me into a small, windowless room with a table, two chairs, and a chalkboard. I wondered if I was going to be interrogated. "Can I get you some coffee?"

"No, thanks," I said. I was already wired from the Coke and chocolate I'd eaten for lunch. Coffee would definitely put me over the edge.

"Tell me about the 727's electrical system," Dan began, tilting back in his chair.

"The electrical system consists of three Westinghouse brushless, air-cooled, engine-driven generators," I recited, without taking a breath. "The generators are rated at forty KVA, one hundred fifteen volts, and four hundred cycles per second."

"That's fine, Kendra," Dan said, laughing. "But let's try to be a little more general. How do the generators work?"

Chuck had wanted us to be specific. I'd studied details. I wasn't even sure I knew how the generators worked.

"Well, when the engines are turning, they turn the generators," I attempted, trying to portray confidence. "And the generators provide electricity to the airplane."

"How does the electricity get from the generators to the airplane?" Dan asked.

"Through generator field relays," I said.

"What does a generator field relay do?"

"It connects the generator to the generator field."

"Can you draw me a picture of the electrical system? It would make it easier for you to explain."

"Draw the whole electrical system?" My mouth fell open in dismay.

"Just a rough sketch," Dan said. "It doesn't have to be perfect. As long as it shows all the buses and how they're connected." He passed me a pad of paper and a pencil.

I stared at the paper and envisioned my whole career going down the toilet. All my training, all my licenses and ratings, and all my experience flight instructing, and flying charter, freight, and for a commuter airline whirling clockwise toward the hole. One flush, and everything would be gone.

"Do you want to take a break?" he asked.

"I just need to think for a few minutes," I said. "I wasn't prepared to *draw* the systems. Chuck said—"

"I wanted to talk to you about Chuck," he interrupted, standing and then sitting down again. "I heard he and your classmates gave you a bit of a hard time."

"How did you hear that?" I asked, looking up from the blank pad. I hadn't told anyone.

"Al mentioned it," Dan said. "Chuck's been having some personal problems lately. We're encouraging him to take a leave of absence."

I gaped at him, too tired to ask the obvious questions. Such as why, if Al had been so aware of what was going on, he hadn't said or done anything to remedy the situation. And why, if Chuck was having personal problems significant enough to warrant a leave of absence, he was still teaching.

"On behalf of the airline, we owe you an apology," he continued. "And if you want to reschedule your whole checkride, I'll be happy to arrange it for you."

I thought about drawing the electrical system. I knew there were nineteen electrical buses, and I knew what they did. If I had them down on paper, I could probably connect them.

"I'd rather get this over with today," I said.

I was carrying my suitcases through the lobby on my way to check out of the hotel when I ran into Brett.

"Congratulations," he said. "I hear you did pretty well on your checkride."

I handed my room key to the clerk behind the desk and went outside to wait for the van to the airport.

"Hey, Kendra," he continued, following me outside. "Can't we be friends again? Ground school is over, and we all made it through."

I looked at my watch, wondering when the van was going to come.

"You know what? They're doing seniority within the class by age now. The oldest is the most senior and on down the line."

The van finally pulled up, and the driver threw my bags in the back.

"It's pretty ironic," he went on. "I studied my ass off to get a good seniority number, and now I'll wind up near the bottom of the class. The four most junior people are going to be sent to Guam! But since Sherman wants to go to Guam anyway, he said he'd bid Cleveland and trade with me."

I climbed into the van.

Brett walked over to the open window.

"By age?" I asked, too stunned by the implications to remember I wasn't talking to Brett. I was the second youngest in the class.

"I know," Brett said. "It's a total bummer."

"And the four youngest are going to *Guam?*" It couldn't be true.

Newark was supposed to be the most understaffed base in the system. Second officers had to be needed there.

"Better go buy a new bathing suit. Listen," he said, getting serious. "Do you think when I come out to Guam in six months we can have dinner together?"

"Maybe," I said, thinking about Guam. All I knew was that it was a tiny island in the western Pacific, that it had been important in World War II, and that now it boasted a large military population. It was not a place I had ever wanted to visit.

"I'll call you as soon as I get out there," he said. "We'll start over."

ABNORMAL PROCEDURES

By the time the first officer arrived at six A.M., I'd already been at the airport for an hour. I'd gotten there early to give myself enough time to read and sign the paperwork for the flight, preflight the interior and exterior of the airplane, get the weather and clearance, program the performance data computer, and check to make sure all 301 switches, knobs, dials, gauges, and lights on the flight engineer panel were positioned, indicating, and working properly.

"Hi," the first officer said, dropping his flight bag into the space between his seat and the window. "I'm Matt."

"I'm Kendra."

"Are you new to Hemisphere or new to Guam?" he asked, climbing into the right seat. He tossed his hat in the direction of the coat closet, balled up his tie and stuffed it into his oxygen mask, and took off his black boots. I noticed he was wearing red socks.

"Both," I said. "This is my first solo trip." I'd been on Guam for three days, having completed my first few initial-operating-experience flights out of Newark. I'd flown two trips from Guam with the second-officer supervisor in order to learn the additional international procedures, and this flight to Manila was my debut as a fully qualified second officer.

"We'll try to make it memorable, then," Matt said, checking the switches on the overhead panel. "Do you know Captain Perrault?"

"No," I said, hefting the twenty-pound book that contained the runway weight limits onto my desk.

"There are only two things you need to know about Brendan Perrault," Matt said. "Don't leave the cockpit, and don't let him catch you sleeping."

"Okay," I said, writing down our maximum takeoff weights for various flap and power settings. That sounded easy enough.

Captain Perrault didn't enter the cockpit until five minutes before departure. I was wearing headphones and trying to copy down the weight and balance information the dispatcher was reading at a rapid-fire pace when he kicked the back of my chair. I immediately moved my seat forward so he could get by, but I didn't get a good look at him until I'd finished with the paperwork and turned around to place it on the pedestal between the two pilot seats.

Brendan Perrault was in his thirties, young for a captain at a major airline, and his uniform was immaculate. His shirt was starched, his shoes were shined, and his sunglasses were without a smudge. The only thing that kept him from looking like an advertisement for the perfect airline pilot was the miniature elephant trunk he was wearing on his nose.

I laughed.

"What the hell is *that?*" Perrault asked Matt, pointing his trunk in my direction.

"That," Matt said, "is our second officer."

Perrault stared at me. "I hate women pilots," he said.

He's joking, I told myself. No one wearing an elephant nose would say something like that seriously. But when he never cracked a smile, I stopped laughing.

"What's the delay here?" he asked Matt. "Tell them we're ready to push."

Matt put on his headset and talked to the ground crew. The tow truck started pushing us back.

"We're cleared to start," Matt said.

"Crank them all," Perrault said, removing his elephant nose and hanging it from the magnetic compass on the windshield.

"Turning one," Matt said, moving the ignition switch to ground start.

Prrrhhht!

It sounded like either Matt or Brendan Perrault had farted. Loudly.

Prrrrrrrrhhhhhht!

So far all of the crews I'd flown with had been respectful and professional. I'd almost put ground school out of my mind.

"Do we have oil pressure or not?" Perrault asked. Since the oil pressure gauge was on my panel, it was my job to call out the rise in oil pressure.

"We've got some kind of pressure," Matt said.

They both laughed.

"Oil pressure is rising," I said.

"It's about time," Perrault said, shaking his head.

"Sorry," I said. "It's my first day."

"That's obvious."

Once the engines were started and I'd put the generators on line, turned on the hydraulic pumps, and regulated the air-conditioning, my next job was to read the captain and first officer the taxi checklist.

"Flaps?" I called.

"Set, five," Matt said.

Prrrhhht!

"Yaw damper?" I continued.

"Checked," Matt said.

Prrrrrrhhhhht!

"Takeoff data and bugs?"

"Checked and set."

Prrhht!

"Controls?"

"Checked."

Prrrrrrrrrrrrrrrhhhhhhht!

"Takeoff briefing?"

Perrault stopped the airplane at the hold line and set the parking brake. "Below a hundred knots, we'll abort for any system malfunction," he said, turning to face me. "After a hundred, I don't want to hear a word from you unless we have an engine failure, a fire, or a loss of all hydraulics."

"Okay," I said. That was a standard takeoff briefing, although I was used to hearing it said in a more civilized way. "Taxi checklist complete."

During takeoff and climb I was too busy monitoring the hydraulic pressures as the gear and flaps were raised, setting the pressurization, cross-feeding the fuel, and calling our times out of the gate and off the ground into operations to notice that the farting sounds had stopped.

"I could sure use a cup of coffee," Perrault said, leveling off at cruising altitude.

I set the throttles to the power setting indicated by the performance computer.

"So could I," Matt agreed. "I wonder when they're going to bring us breakfast."

"Don't reduce that power until we've gotten our airspeed!" Perrault yelled, pushing the throttles back to climb power.

"Sorry," I said. I'd been taught to set cruise power as soon as we leveled off.

"Yesterday, we didn't get anything to eat until we'd started our descent into Tokyo," Perrault continued.

"The service is getting worse and worse around here," Matt commented, sliding his seat back and putting his red-socked feet up on the instrument panel.

"Did I tell you I found a house?" Perrault asked Matt.

"In Houston?"

"River Oaks. Five bedrooms, a lap pool in the backyard, a Jacuzzi on the deck . . ."

While they were talking, I watched my panel intently. Once I'd set cruise power, I only had to perform two functions: control the cockpit and cabin temperatures so that no one complained, and make sure none of the panel's yellow or (God forbid) red lights illuminated.

"Look at that," Perrault said. "You can tell she's a new second officer by the way she's baby-sitting the panel."

"That'll last about a week," Matt said.

"I'm going to the back," Perrault announced. "You still want that coffee?"

"Black with two sugars."

Perrault climbed out of his seat, adjusted his tie in the mirror on the cockpit door, and left for the galley. His elephant trunk stayed in the cockpit.

Matt turned around.

"How's it going?" he asked, suddenly friendly. "You've been awfully quiet."

"Does he hate me for any special reason?" I asked, studying my panel. I was feeding fuel to all three engines from the center tank. As soon as the tanks were even I'd have to flip various switches to allow each tank to feed fuel to its respective engine.

"Who, Brendan?"

I nodded.

"He doesn't hate you," Matt said.

"Am I doing something wrong?"

"You're doing fine."

"Then why is he treating me this way?"

"He just kind of . . . marches to a different drummer," Matt said. "Don't worry about it.

A few minutes later I saw smoke wafting in from under the door.

"I think we've got a problem," I informed Matt with professional calm.

Matt turned around to look. "You better go check it out."

It was fortunate I'd recently been trained in emergency procedures, I thought, putting on my oxygen mask and smoke goggles. I armed myself with the fire extinguisher and heroically threw open the cockpit door.

But instead of confronting a raging fire, I found myself looking down the aisle at a hundred and sixty-three fascinated Filipinos. The only sign of smoke was a coffee cup filled with steaming dry ice on the floor just outside the door.

I retreated back into the cockpit. I hung up my oxygen mask, took off the smoke goggles, and replaced the fire extinguisher on the back wall.

"Did you put out the fire?" Matt asked, barely suppressing a grin.

"It burned itself out," I said, wanting to lay my head down on my desk.

"Look at the bright side," Matt said. "You'll probably never see those passengers again."

"Coffee call," Perrault announced, entering the cockpit with his key. "How's the panel?"

"Fine," I said.

"Don't take your eyes off it," he instructed, climbing into his seat. "You never know what might happen." He looked at Matt and smiled.

I fine-tuned the throttles, scanned the panel, and settled lower into my chair. The day had barely begun, and already I was exhausted. It had been a twenty-hour flight across nine time zones from Boston to Guam (not including the time spent changing planes in Houston, San Francisco, and Honolulu), and I still wasn't over my jet lag.

I was jolted awake by loud knocking. Since I sat closest to the door, it was my job to respond to all knocks. I jumped out of my seat and looked through the peephole. It was one of the flight attendants with our breakfast. I let her in.

"Hi, guys," she said, putting down three trays on my desk. "We have eggs, cereal, and French toast. What do you want to drink?"

"I'll have another cup of black coffee," Perrault said, taking the tray with cereal off my desk.

"I'll have orange juice," Matt said, taking the tray with French toast.

"And what about you?" she asked me.

I was examining the yellow-and-brown congealed mess that was supposedly scrambled eggs. "Orange juice, please," I said.

"Be right back," she said, bouncing out of the cockpit.

"What's her name?" Matt asked.

"Yvette," Perrault said, his mouth full of cornflakes. "Cute, isn't she?"

"Adorable."

"She's got a good sense of humor, too."

I bit into my roll. It was rubbery and hard to chew.

When Yvette knocked, I got up to let her in again. She handed Matt and me our juices and Perrault his coffee.

"Thanks, honey," Perrault said. "Why don't you visit for a while?"

"I guess I could—for a few minutes," Yvette said, sitting on the jump seat. "It's not too bad back there today. Most of them are sleeping or reading."

Prrrhhht!

"Brendan!" Yvette scolded.

Prrrhhht!

"I hope that's coming from your fart bag and not you," she said.

Fart bag?

Prrrhhht!

"Let me have it," Yvette demanded. "I want to show it to Linda in the back."

Perrault handed Yvette what looked like a plastic toy, and she left the cockpit.

Perrault and Matt looked at each other, smiled, and looked at me.

"I guess I should be relieved it's not contagious," I told them.

On every flight over two hours the second officer is required to record cruise engine temperatures in a metal-covered logbook. Some of the readings are taken from the second officer panel, but most come from the central panel located between the captain and first officer. In order to read the gauges, I had to lean forward between Brendan and Matt.

"I've got a good one for you," Perrault told Matt over my head. "How many sideways seats are there on a 727?"

I copied down the EPR and EGT readings in the logbook.

"I give up," Matt responded.

"Four. Three toilets and the second officer's chair."

Matt laughed.

I copied down the N1 and N2 readings.

"How many second officers does it take to screw in a lightbulb?" Matt asked.

"I don't know," Perrault said.

"Five. One to hold the bulb and four to turn the panel."

"I like it." Perrault laughed.

I returned to my desk to complete the readings.

"What the hell happened to the oil in number two?" Perrault bellowed.

I looked up from the logbook. The oil quantity gauge for the number two engine was indicating zero. There were four gallons when we'd started.

"I don't know," I answered.

"How long has it been like that?" he demanded.

That was a good question. When was my last scan? Before I fell asleep, I realized. Because Yvette woke me up, then we had breakfast, and then I started on the engine readings. . . .

"I know it had four gallons—"

"When did it have four gallons? How long has it been leaking? You're supposed to keep track of those things! That's what you're paid for!" Perrault yelled.

"It must have happened during breakfast," I said. "I wasn't watching carefully enough." This was it. I was going to be fired on my first day. I could have cried.

"Well, what are we going to do?" he asked, calmer.

"I'll look up the abnormal," I offered. As a second officer, I was required to carry around a six-inch-thick manual that detailed what to do in any emergency or abnormal situation. I pulled the manual out of my flight bag and began paging through it.

"Oil quantity indicating zero," I read when I found the right page. "Check circuit breaker." There were two full walls of circuit breakers in the cockpit of a 727. All I had to do was find the one that controlled the number two engine's oil quantity.

I decided to search systematically. I would start at the top of the wall behind Perrault's seat and work my way down.

Perrault and Matt watched with amusement.

"Notice anything about those circuit breakers?" Perrault asked.

"Like maybe they all pertain to the passenger cabin?" Matt added.

I cursed myself. I'd known that from training, of course. I moved my search over to the other wall, which pertained to the major aircraft systems, and eventually found the circuit breaker for the number two engine oil-quantity gauge. It was popped. I went back to my checklist.

"A popped circuit breaker may be reset once," I read. I pushed the circuit breaker in. The oil quantity gauge went back to four gallons.

"Abnormal resolved," Perrault said.

"I'm really sorry," I said. "I don't know how I could have missed such an obvious thing—"

"Maybe you learned something," Perrault said. "Maybe you won't sleep on the job again." He and Matt laughed.

"*I've* certainly never fallen asleep in the cockpit," Matt said. They laughed harder.

I slunk lower in my sideways seat, wishing I could disappear.

When we finally arrived at the gate in Manila, Perrault and Matt fought over the mirror on the cockpit door as they combed their hair and straightened their ties.

"If you leave the cockpit, make sure to lock the door behind you," Perrault mentioned. "This is a poor country. They'll steal anything that isn't bolted down."

I had to leave the cockpit to do my walk-around inspection, but I made certain the door was locked.

In the cabin I was greeted by fourteen aircraft cleaners, six caterers, and four supervisors.

"Good morning, ma'am," they said, almost in unison.

"Good morning," I answered.

"Did you have a nice flight?" one of the supervisors asked. He was standing in the forward galley eating honey-roasted peanuts with the Hemisphere logo on the package.

"It was okay," I said.

"Are you going shopping?"

"No, just outside to check the airplane."

"Too bad," he said. "My cousin owns the electronics store, and he is having a good sale of car stereos."

"I don't have a car," I said. For my first week, Hemisphere had put me up at the Guam Hilton (which had a van that went back and forth to the airport), but after Friday I was going to have to find a place to live and a car to drive. Unless I could manage to work out a base trade with someone in Newark.

"This is a special one-time deal," he said, shaking his head. "You can buy the car stereo now and save it until you get a car."

"Maybe next time," I said.

At the bottom of the jetway stairs there was a soldier with a machine gun slung over his shoulder who was also eating honey-roasted peanuts. I nodded to him, did a quick walk-around, and returned to the cockpit. Everything seemed to be in place.

Perrault came back while I was filling out the weight-and-balance form.

"Looks like we're getting line-checked," he said. That meant an FAA inspector was going to ride along in the cockpit and evaluate our performance. "It would be better for all of us if you acted like you knew what you were doing."

"If I'm doing something fundamentally wrong, I wish you'd tell me," I said, turning around. "Otherwise I won't be able to correct it."

"Oh, I'd tell you," Perrault said, settling into his seat. "Don't worry about that."

A few minutes later Matt returned to the cockpit with a middle-aged man.

"Lester Daniels, FAA," the man said, shaking my hand. Daniels was bald on top, and his remaining gray hair was slicked back with some sort of grease. His FAA ID was attached to the pocket of his green aloha shirt, which was so tight across his stomach I thought the buttons were going to pop.

I listened to the updated weather, finished the weight and balance, compared the fuel slip to the fuel gauges, and tried to pretend that Lester Daniels, FAA, wasn't sitting in the jump seat behind me.

"Delayed start on three," Perrault said, after we'd started engines one and two.

A delayed engine start was a fuel-conserving technique. Since two engines provided more than enough power to taxi, many captains elected not to start the third engine until just before takeoff. There were only two problems with a delayed engine start: it would double my workload at the busiest possible time, and I'd never done one before.

"Taxi check," Perrault called as I was trying to find the delayed-engine-start checklist I knew was somewhere in my flight bag.

"Stand by," I said, giving up my search. I hadn't even done my after-start flow. I put the generators for engines one and two on line and switched essential power to engine two. I couldn't remember if I was supposed to turn off one of the B-hydraulic pumps or not. I didn't want to overload the electrical system, so I turned one off just to be safe. Next I came to the air-conditioning. Was I was supposed to use air from the APU for both air-conditioning packs or use air from the number one engine for just the left pack? Using air from the number one engine for the left pack (which provided air-conditioning to the cockpit only) was normal procedure until the APU was shut off, but the APU was going to have to stay on until we started the number three engine. With only the left pack on, the passengers were going to get very hot. But it was better to be safe than sorry. I mentally apologized to the passengers, shut off the APU air, and put on just the left pack.

"Taxi check!" Perrault called again.

I was only halfway through the checklist before Perrault called to start engine three. I hurriedly shut off the pack, opened the APU bleed switches, and waited for the duct pressure to reach the minimum for engine start.

"Can I see your licenses and medical certificate?" Daniels asked me.

I looked at him with disbelief. Couldn't he see this wasn't the best time to ask?

"Do we have oil pressure?" Perrault asked.

"Oil pressure is rising," I said. I'd missed the call again.

"Thank you," Perrault said.

"I'll have to show you later," I told Daniels.

"Start valve?" Perrault asked.

The pneumatic duct pressure gauge was on my panel, and I was supposed to be monitoring the duct pressure during start. When the start valve opened it decreased, and when the start valve closed it increased. If the second officer didn't call out "start valve closed" upon seeing an increase in duct pressure, the captain would assume the start valve was still open and take emergency action.

"Start valve is closed," I said.

Perrault shook his head and asked for the rest of the taxi check.

I had to tell him to stand by again while I went through the after-start flow on the panel.

Fortunately, air traffic control gave us a five-minute delay at the end of the runway, and I had time to get everything done and even give Daniels a briefing on how to work his seat belt and where to find his oxygen mask.

After a normal takeoff, I turned to my panel to check the hydraulics and set the pressurization.

"Where's the goddamn gear crank?" Daniels suddenly shouted.

The gear crank was considered essential emergency equipment. If, for any number of reasons, there wasn't enough hydraulic pressure to lower the landing gear, the second officer could, using the gear crank and brute strength, still get the gear down and locked.

The gear crank normally occupied a spot on the back wall of the cockpit between the crash ax and fire extinguisher. It had been there during my morning preflight. I'd definitely seen it. But now the spot on the wall was empty, and I couldn't remember if I had actually checked it again in Manila.

"That gear crank is *required!*" Daniels yelled.

Perrault turned around. He looked at the empty spot on the wall, and he looked at me. "Where's the gear crank, Kendra?" he asked in an ominous tone of voice.

I searched the back of the cockpit. I looked in the seat pocket behind my seat and inside my desk. I dumped out my flight bag and checked my backpack. But I couldn't find it.

"What did I tell you about locking the door in Manila?" Perrault asked as if he were talking to a naughty child.

"I locked the door in Manila," I said.

And then it all began to make sense. Matt's comments about never leaving the cockpit. Perrault's point about locking the door in Manila. I suddenly understood what had happened. Perrault had waited until I went outside to do my walk-around. Then he'd entered the cockpit and hidden the gear crank. He'd planned to play another joke on me, but it had backfired because Lester Daniels, FAA, had noticed the missing gear crank before Perrault could put it back. And now, I thought, savoring the irony, Perrault was going to get a violation because he was the captain and therefore responsible! This was too good to be true.

"You didn't happen to notice the gear crank up there, did you?" I asked Perrault as subtly as I could.

"I think it might have fallen behind those books," Perrault said nonchalantly. There was a stack of manuals beside Perrault's seat, and I climbed around Daniels to look through them. Sure enough, the gear crank was buried underneath. I hung it back on the wall.

"Another crisis averted," Matt said. He and Perrault looked at each other.

"I want to see all your certificates *now*," Daniels told the three of us.

We handed them over, and he pulled a small notebook and pen out of one of the pockets of his aloha shirt.

"You know, I'm getting a little tired of the sloppy flying I see going on at Hemisphere," Daniels said. "You people think that out here in the middle of the Pacific the FAA can't find you. But you're wrong! The FAA can find you *anywhere*." He finished copying down our names and license numbers and returned our certificates. "And what the hell is that?" he asked, pointing to Perrault's elephant nose. "Do you actually call yourselves *professionals?*" He shook his head in disgust. "I'm going to the back to have some lunch and think about what I've just seen and what I'm going to do about it." He got up and left the cockpit.

Perrault and Matt started laughing hysterically.

"He could revoke our licenses," I said, not understanding how they could laugh at a time like this.

That only made them laugh harder. Matt turned as red as his socks, and Perrault had tears running down his face.

"I don't understand what's so funny," I said angrily. The more they laughed, the angrier I became. "You've done everything possible to make my first day miserable! Embarrassing me with the fart bag, humiliating me in front of the passengers with the dry ice, putting me on the spot with the FAA! Why are you doing this?"

Perrault and Matt stopped laughing. Perrault got out of his seat and sat down in the jump seat behind me. He swiveled my chair around so I was facing him.

"We have something to tell you, Kendra," he said seriously.

Matt started to laugh again, but Perrault kicked him.

"Everyone who's been in Guam for over a week knows Lester Daniels. He does work for the FAA, but not as an inspector. He's an air traffic controller in Guam Center."

I stared at Perrault, not fully comprehending what he was saying.

"Lester flies to Manila whenever he gets a few days off," Perrault continued. "Because he's a controller, he has jump seat privileges. If you hadn't been brand-new out here, we never could have played this little joke on you because you would have recognized his voice." He studied me to see if I understood.

"You mean you set the whole thing up?" I asked.

"We couldn't resist," he said, smiling.

"You assholes!" I started to laugh and cry at the same time.

Perrault put his arm around my shoulder and squeezed it gently.

"Welcome to Guam, Kendra," he said. "You're going to love it out here."

WEATHER

Three days after her arrival on Guam, my mother was ready to continue to New Zealand and Australia (courtesy of Hemisphere's generous pass program which enabled parents—and stepparents—spouses, and children of pilots to fly space available anywhere in the Hemisphere system for a five dollar service charge). The island's only bookstore, she complained, had more varieties of "Jesus loves you" bookmarks than books. The hotel's "gourmet" restaurant had garnished her salad with a dead cockroach. The beach had signs saying a broken sewage pipe made the water unsafe for swimming. There weren't any artisans with interesting crafts to sell. The military was everywhere. How could she have let me come to this intellectual and cultural wasteland, this *paved rock* in the middle of the Pacific? What if, God forbid, I ever needed emergency surgery?

She certainly couldn't allow me to be treated in that pathetic excuse for a hospital where all the so-called medical professionals had been trained in Third World countries (an observation she'd made when we'd rushed Norman to the emergency room to have a welt on his arm examined because she was certain it was a poisonous spider bite—it wasn't). I would have to be airlifted to a suitable teaching hospital, but Guam was so far away from civilization (eight flying hours southwest of Honolulu, six hours north of Sydney, three hours south of Tokyo), I would probably die en route. She couldn't stand even thinking about it!

A sentiment she chose to share—to my utter mortification—with the chief pilot, who we'd encountered in the Rexall drugstore (Guam being such a "small town") where my mother had been buying zinc oxide to put on over her number 45 sunblock because she was convinced that the combination of equatorial sun and the depleted ozone layer would cause skin cancer.

She was very pleased to meet him, my mother told the chief pilot after I'd been forced to introduce them. Hemisphere's Guam operation seemed very well run, she said, and she was sure *some* of the pilots were well suited for island life. But her daughter wasn't one of them, and he would simply have to do his absolute best to have me transferred back to the East Coast as soon as possible.

To which the chief pilot responded that he was quite aware of my desire to change domiciles (since almost every day I asked him how my base trade was coming along), and my mother had his complete assurance that the first available slot in Newark was mine.

What he'd neglected to mention, though, was that no matter how many open slots there were in Newark, he wasn't letting me go anywhere until my replacement arrived on the island.

∞

Which is how I came to be flying a round trip between Guam and Nagoya, Japan, two months later on the morning Typhoon Roger was advancing toward Guam from five hundred miles to the southeast.

"Is Roger going to be your first typhoon?" Marshall, the captain, asked, opening his Mickey Mouse lunch box, the only kind of lunch box you could buy on Guam (because all the stores catered to tourists, and all the tourists wanted Mickey Mouse).

"Yes," I answered, looking up from the crossword puzzle I was working on. Aside from periodically scanning the panel, there wasn't much else to do on a three-hour flight over water. "I've only been out here for eight months." And two weeks and four days. Not that I was counting.

"The last typhoon was about a year ago," David, the first officer, said, watching Marshall line up six plastic containers on the instrument panel. "It took a week to get the electricity back."

"That's why I invested in a generator," Marshall said, tucking a napkin into his collar. Marshall was short, round, and bald, and he'd been flying for Hemisphere for over thirty years, the last five of which had been out of Guam. "With the generator and the cistern, we won't have to worry." He opened a container of granola and poured it into a container of yogurt.

"Why do you need a cistern?" I asked.

"Whenever the electricity goes out, the water goes, too," he said, consuming his yogurt-granola mix in three bites and putting the empty containers back into his lunch box.

"How do you take showers?" I asked in horror. I could live without electricity, but I couldn't imagine enduring Guam's extreme heat and humidity without showers.

"You go swimming," David said. "And you make sure you have a good supply of bottled water for drinking and full bathtubs for flushing the toilets."

"Either of you interested in these prunes?" Marshall asked, opening another container and sniffing with disgust. "I swear, Molly wants me to spend the whole flight in the little blue room."

"No, thanks," I said, thinking longingly of the Northeast with its interminable winters and chronic air traffic control delays.

"Those muffins look pretty good," David said.

"I'm not offering my muffins," Marshall said, biting into one possessively. "Why don't you ever bring your own food?"

"It's more fun to eat yours," David said.

Marshall laughed. Marshall, David, and I had been flying together for three weeks. Marshall always brought food, and David always drooled over it.

"What do you think this is?" Marshall asked, holding up a container shaped like a drinking glass. "It looks like some of that health food stuff." He passed it over to me, knowing David would want to taste it.

I opened the top and sniffed. It was cold, white, frothy, and had no smell. "I think it's a tofu milk shake," I said, handing it back.

"I don't know what's come over that woman," Marshall said, shaking his head. "She used to pack me cinnamon rolls and apple turnovers. Now I get bran muffins and tofu milk shakes. It's almost enough to make a man lose his appetite."

We both knew Marshall would eat every drop of the food his wife had packed plus the crew meals that would be served on the flight.

"If you ever lose your appetite, I'll be the first to call the ambulance," David said.

∞

Our schedule called for forty-five minutes on the ground in Nagoya, and Marshall and David decided to go into the terminal to see what they could find to eat. I finished some paperwork, then performed my walk-around inspection. When I returned to the cockpit, boarding was in progress.

No sooner had I sat down and taken out my calculator to convert the fuel from liters to gallons to pounds than a dozen passengers barged into the cockpit armed with still and video cameras. They removed Marshall's and David's hats from the hooks on the back wall and took turns taking pictures of every person wearing a hat and sitting in one of the pilot seats.

Then they smiled, spoke excitedly in Japanese, and pulled me to my feet. They put Marshall's hat on my head and positioned themselves next to me. There were no woman airline pilots in Japan, and I had gotten used to being a source of curiosity. I knew that no matter how busy I appeared to be, the passengers would insist on taking my picture. I dutifully smiled for all twelve cameras, and wondered idly how many Japanese photo albums I was in.

"Guam's in condition three," David announced, entering the cockpit with the latest weather information. Typhoon condition three meant a typhoon could hit within forty-eight hours.

"I'm sure glad we're off tomorrow," Marshall said, arranging his food purchases on the instrument panel. He fastened his seat belt, checked the switches and instruments on his side of the cockpit, and unwrapped a plate of sushi.

"I'm on reserve," David said, watching Marshall chew. If he had bought any food for himself, he'd already eaten it.

"How did you get stuck with reserve?" Marshall asked, expertly using chopsticks to pick up a slice of raw fish. Our schedules generally had the same captain, first officer, and second officer flying together for the entire month.

"I needed next Thursday off to get a couple of the dogs spayed, so I had to take whatever the scheduler had." David adopted stray dogs, of which there were thousands on Guam. He had them spayed or neutered, got them their shots, and kept them in his house and yard. At last count he had over twenty.

"What happens to the airplanes in a typhoon?" I asked. Hemisphere had eight 727s and three DC-10s based on Guam and no hangars.

"If they're out, they stay where they are until it passes," David said. "If they're on Guam, they get flown to the closest place with better weather."

"Who flies them?" I asked.

"Whoever's available," David said. "And in a typhoon, the scheduler considers any pilot who answers the phone available."

"I'll remember not to answer my phone," I said.

The weather in Guam was clear, and the wind was calm.

"It doesn't look like a typhoon is coming," I commented as we started our descent.

"The lighting is different," Marshall said. "It'll be more obvious on the ground."

"Do you have a camera?" David asked me. "This is great weather for photography. The ominous calm before the storm—"

"I'm spending my ominous calm playing golf," Marshall said. "I'd like to get in nine holes this afternoon. Who knows what condition the course will be in after the typhoon!"

∞

The three bedroom apartment I shared with four other woman pilots was in Tumon (tourist haven, but convenient to the airport), sandwiched between the Romeo and Juliet Honeymoon Hotel and the Buffalo Bill Saloon and Gun Club. The hotel advertised suites with pink heart-shaped bathtubs and discounted tickets to Buffalo Bill's. The saloon advertised cowboy, cowgirl, and Indian costumes for dress up and picture taking, Wild West outlaw targets for shooting, and a bar for drinking, smoking, and acting out simulated brawls. Fortunately, the shooting took place in soundproof booths and the revelers usually returned to their suites by ten.

"Did you hear about the typhoon?" I asked Meg, the only roommate who lived on Guam (the other three—a DC-10 second officer and two 727 first officers—commuted from Hawaii and only stayed with us a few nights a month). I dropped my flight bag by the door, kicked off my shoes, and looked over to see what she was watching on her portable four-inch color TV.

"What typhoon?" she asked, rubbing her eyes and stretching. It was three-thirty, and she was lying on the couch, still in her nightgown.

"Typhoon Roger," I said, noting that the local TV station was broadcasting the same (pirated) CNN segment they'd shown last night. "We're in condition three."

"That's a bummer," she said. "I'm supposed to fly to Tokyo tomorrow."

"Better bring an overnight bag," I said, heading into my room to change out of my uniform. "I'm going over to Gibson's to get typhoon supplies. Do you want to come?"

"Just let me get dressed," she said, turning off the TV.

∞

Gibson's was Guam's equivalent of Kmart (without the discounts), a huge, L-shaped, warehouselike structure, selling everything from appliances to groceries to fine china to clothing.

"I'm thinking of buying a VCR," Meg said as we loaded our cart with bottled water. The store was packed with both residents stocking up for the typhoon and tourists on their regular tour-bus stop (the attraction seemed to be the Gibson's motto, "American goods at American prices"). "I want to be able to rent movies instead of watching TV all the time."

"There aren't any decent movies to rent," I said. The video stores on Guam specialized in two kinds of films: action and pornographic.

"You never know," she said. "I'll meet you at the register." Since there wasn't a lot (that we would want) to buy on Guam, and since our travel off-island was free, Meg was always looking for ways to spend her money.

I grabbed the last two rolls of masking tape off the shelf and ten votive candles (the only kind left) and got in the checkout line behind eight giggling tourists. Their carts were stuffed with Mickey Mouse beach towels, Mickey Mouse nightshirts, complete sets of golf clubs in Mickey Mouse golf bags, and entire cartons of potato chips.

"I got the deluxe model," Meg said, rolling up her cart next to mine. She cut ahead of several tourists, but they just smiled at her. "It has a fourteen-day programmable memory, a remote control, and it can be used with batteries."

"That's probably a hundred dollars worth of batteries," I commented, seeing that her cart was filled with D-cell Evereadys.

"I know," she said. "But when the power goes out, and everyone else is sitting around in the dark twiddling their thumbs, we can be watching movies!"

∞

We loaded our purchases into my Guam Bomb—a rusty, seven-year-old Toyota I'd bought for three hundred dollars—and drove back to the apartment. While Meg worked on setting up her VCR, I walked the one block to the beach to take pictures. Tumon Bay was only four feet deep and protected by a reef, so there weren't usually any waves. But today there were whitecaps inside the reef, and the waterline seemed higher up on the sand. The sky was still clear, but the sunlight was much deeper than normal and tinged with yellow.

Meg and I ate dinner in front of the TV. The local news informed us that Typhoon Roger had accelerated, and Guam was now in condition two. After dinner we taped Xs on all the windows and watched the first half of *Gone with the Wind* on the VCR. Meg, to my surprise, had found it in one of the local video stores. But the store, in typical Guam fashion, had only had the first half. We said goodnight at eleven, and just as I was falling asleep, I thought I heard the faintest whispers of wind.

When I woke up the sky was overcast with the darkest clouds I'd ever seen, the wind was rattling the windows, and the radio said we were in condition one. Meg had already left for Tokyo with her overnight bag. I didn't envy her flying in this weather, and I was glad I was off, but I wished one of our other roommates was with me in the apartment. I wasn't anxious to experience my first typhoon alone.

I showered (lest it be my last opportunity), made breakfast, put a load of laundry into the washing machine, and settled on the couch to write more letters to management personnel trying to find a way to get off Guam.

At eleven, the radio said Roger was heading straight for us and would likely pass overhead at six in the evening.

At noon, the rain began. It came in horizontal sheets, and it wasn't long before it began seeping into the living room through the base of the sliding glass doors. I moved the furniture as far away as possible and packed towels against the glass, but the water soon soaked through.

At one, the electricity went out.

At two, the taps ran dry.

By three, the living room was under an inch of water that was heading for the bedrooms. I took everything I could move off the floor and put it on the beds.

At three-thirty, I was reading by the light of a votive candle, when I heard someone pounding on the door. At first I thought it was the wind, but then I saw David's face in the window. I opened the door, and more water flooded in.

"Get your flight bag," he said, shaking water off his poncho. "There's one more airplane left, and we need a second officer to take it to Yap."

"The scheduler hasn't called," I said, happy to see another human being. "So I'm not available."

"The scheduler asked me to knock on doors," David said. "Since you answered your door, you're obligated to help us out."

"There's no way I'm getting in an airplane in the middle of a typhoon—"

"If you'd hurry up, we'd be able to take off before the typhoon hits," David said. "Anyway, it'll be safer in the airplane than on the ground. Down here you could get hit with flying glass, crushed by a falling tree, smothered in a collapsed building—"

"Who's the captain?" I asked, resigning myself.

"Marshall," David said, smiling. "He was also stupid enough to answer his door."

"At least the wind's straight down the runway," Marshall said when David and I staggered, dripping, into the cockpit. "I want everything strapped down before takeoff. The last thing we need is for one of us to get hit with a fifty-pound flight bag. The first three thousand feet are going to be the most critical. Once we get some altitude and start heading away from the typhoon, the turbulence should taper off."

"Okay," I said, strapping down my flight bag.

"They're ready to push," David announced. He was using hand signals instead of the intercom to talk to the mechanics below because the wind and rain were too severe for them to plug in their headsets.

"Let's go, then," Marshall said. "The weather's not going to get any better while we wait."

Taking off into the typhoon was terrifying. The wind, which had been a steady fifty knots straight down the runway, suddenly shifted, leaving us to cope with a crosswind that, had there been time for me to look up the component, would definitely have exceeded the airplane's limitations. Marshall had to use full aileron and rudder deflection just to keep us on the runway and on all three wheels. Although we had the windshield wipers on high, they were no match for the blowing rain, and Marshall was forced to use his side window to see where we were going.

When we finally lurched into the air, the turbulence was unbeliev-able. It took the combined strength of Marshall and David just to keep the wings level. The airplane climbed and descended with a will of its own, and Marshall steered us directly over the water so we

wouldn't be in danger of hitting anything. Even though we'd supposedly tied everything down, manuals, smoke goggles, checklists, and
life jackets flew through the cockpit. Lightning flashed continuously
in all the windows, and rain pelted the windshield. If I hadn't been
so busy monitoring the engine gauges for possible engine flameouts
due to water ingestion, alternating the ignition switches every ten
minutes, and catching flying objects, I would have been paralyzed
with fright.

Climbing out of twenty thousand feet, the turbulence abated, and
Marshall reached for his lunch box. I went to work on one of last
month's *New York Times* crossword puzzles that had been sent (along
with the usual packet of aviation disaster articles) by my mother.

"What's for supper?" David asked.

"Looks like pasta salad," Marshall said, opening the first container
and putting it on the instrument panel. He removed three more
containers. "Sliced chicken, zucchini bread, and carrot sticks."

"That's all?" David asked.

"Molly didn't have much time," he said. "I wasn't supposed to
be flying today, as you know."

"I'm pretty hungry myself," David said. "I think I forgot to have
lunch."

"I have no sympathy," Marshall said, moving the containers closer
to his side of the panel. "If it wasn't for you, I'd be home with Molly
enjoying a romantic candlelit dinner."

We landed in Yap at sunset. The wind was calm, and only a
high, thin overcast in the east indicated a typhoon was raging five
hundred miles away.

"Guam says the typhoon is passing and you should come home,"

Hemisphere's agent said when we arrived in operations, a thatched-roof shack which housed a desk, a radio, and a car. The car's battery seemed to be the radio's only power source. "They want to talk to you on the radio."

"How could the typhoon be passing already?" I asked. "We left there less than two hours ago."

"We took off at its height," Marshall said, picking up the microphone.

I glared at David, who had undoubtedly known that when he'd come to get me.

He shrugged.

Although Guam dispatch wanted us to bring the airplane back immediately, Marshall said we weren't flying back through the same horrible weather. He told them we'd stay put for at least two hours and call again for an update. While we waited, he said to David and me, we'd just have to go find ourselves something good to eat.

We landed back in Guam at eleven-thirty. Although the wind was still gusting, it wasn't as strong, and stars could be seen through breaks in the clouds. David dropped me off at the apartment, and I unlocked the door to find Meg on the couch in front of the TV.

"When did you get back?" I asked, sloshing through the water to get close enough to see the screen.

"About an hour ago," she said. "We had a pretty good day. We took the train into the city, walked around, had lunch, saw some sights. . . . I thought you were off today."

"David showed up at the door and said they were desperate, so I had no choice," I said, looking at the TV. "Isn't this the second part of *Gone with the Wind*?"

"Yup," she said. "I found it in the video store at the airport in Tokyo. The captain is flying back there tomorrow and said he'd return it. Do you want me to rewind it?"

"That's okay," I said, pulling one of the chairs up to the TV. "I don't want you to use up the batteries. We don't know how long the power will be out."

As we watched Scarlett rip down the curtains to make a dress, lights began to go on in the hotels along the bay. Soon, the buildings on the hill were illuminated. Finally, lights from Buffalo Bill's and Romeo and Juliet brightened the living room.

We could have turned on our own lights and plugged in the TV and VCR, but it seemed more fitting to watch the rest of *Gone with the Wind* in the dark with battery power.

SLOW FLIGHT

When the phone rang, I was sitting on my suitcase forcing the zipper with one hand, stuffing recalcitrant clothes in with the other, and counting the minutes (one thousand five hundred and sixty-seven) until I departed Guam forever. My transfer to Newark had finally come through, and I was ecstatically heading back to Boston. Back to friends, first-run movies, vegetarian restaurants, phones without static, and electricity that stayed on. Back to winter, spring, and fall, my own furniture, and my hundreds of books.

Back also to my mother and her assumption that my return meant my "seven-year stint of finding myself" (or my delayed adolescent rebellion, break with reality, career confusion, or any of the other excuses she'd used to deny that I was—and had *chosen* to be—a pilot) had come to an end. I was now, she believed, going to fulfill her expectations by cheerfully enrolling in graduate school, marrying a nice pediatrician (who Karen—now in the first year of a pediatric endocrinology fellowship—would introduce me to), having children, and never going near the cockpit of an airplane again.

A delusion I chose not to contradict because I didn't want one of my mother's tantrums to spoil my euphoria about leaving Guam (and there would definitely be a tantrum when I told her I wouldn't be able to fit in graduate school with my new schedule of commuting to Newark to fly my trips and studying in preparation for my upgrade to first officer on the 737, the position I'd been awarded on the last system bid).

I was so busy rhapsodizing about my new life that I picked up the phone without waiting for the answering machine to screen the call.

"How would you like to take off seven hours earlier?" the scheduling dispatcher asked.

"How could I do that?" I responded, suspiciously. The next DC-10 flight to Honolulu wasn't until tomorrow at seven in the evening.

"You could take the Atoll Local," he suggested.

I laughed. The Atoll Local was a twice-weekly trip flown in an old, battered, half-cargo, half-passenger 727-100. It departed Guam at noon, stopped on five remote islands, and was scheduled to land in Honolulu fifteen hours later—the same time as the DC-10. No one would give up the dinner, movie, fully reclining seat, and soft blanket of first class on the DC-10 (where employees could travel if there were open seats) for the Atoll Local.

"I'm serious," the scheduler continued. "I need a second officer for tomorrow's trip. Since you're going to Honolulu anyway, and since you're so anxious to be on your way, I figured you'd jump at the chance to defect sooner and make an extra four hundred dollars in the process."

"No, thanks," I said, watching clothes ooze out of my suitcase onto the floor. I had no intention of jeopardizing my long-awaited escape from exile on a flight that was prone to disaster and delay.

"We don't have anyone else," the scheduler said.

"Sorry," I said. "I'm not feeling well. I think I'm coming down with something."

"The only thing you're coming down with is island fever," he said.

"You're right," I said. "A terrible case. An *incapacitating* case." I'd had island fever since stepping off the DC-10 at Guam International Airport a year and a half ago, which I'd barely kept under control by traveling off-island every time I had a few days free. But ever since the going-away party Meg had thrown for me two nights ago, and ever since selling my car, turning in my airport ID, and allowing my successor to start moving her things into my room in the apartment, it had become acute. I was shaky and panicky, plagued by daydreams and nightmares of the chief pilot rescinding my transfer, imprisoning me on the island forever. "And the only cure is the DC-10."

"The only cure is getting off Guam," he countered. "So try to think of your *assignment* to the Atoll Local as a gift, an expression of our sincere concern for your health, and a symbol of our generosity in fulfilling your wishes to be en route to Newark as quickly as possible."

A gift I didn't want. A gift that kept on giving more of what I didn't want. Starting with the mechanic not showing up.

"What's the plan?" Neil, the tan and blond captain (who bore a striking resemblance to a Malibu Ken doll), asked the dispatcher over the radio. Neil had transferred to Guam from California two weeks before. This would be his first Atoll Local, which, added to the absent mechanic, was not an auspicious beginning.

"You're going anyway," the dispatcher said. Because the airports on the Atoll Local route had neither mechanics, maintenance facilities, nor spare parts, it was customary for Hemisphere to send a mechanic and a kit of parts along on each Atoll Local flight. "And we'll hope for the best."

"Roger that," Neil said.

"A typical Atoll Loco," Duncan, the first officer, said, wiping the sweat off his face with his tie. The 727-100 was only capable of supplying air-conditioning to either the cockpit *or* the passenger cabin while on the ground. Since the passengers were paying, they got the coolest air. "Cursed from the start, guaranteed to make you crazy by the end."

"I wish you wouldn't make comments like that," I said. "I'm nervous enough about this trip."

"Why are you nervous?" Neil asked, thumbing through a surfing magazine.

"Because strange, mysterious, and crazy things always happen on the Atoll Local," Duncan told him. "You've heard of the Bermuda Triangle? Well, this route is the Pacific equivalent."

"Don't jinx us!" I said, hitting him over the head with my plastic checklist.

"I don't get it," Neil said, wrinkling his forehead.

"I've been trying to get out of Guam for a year and a half," I explained. "Now, just when I'm finally staffed in Newark, just when I should be flying nonstop to Honolulu on a positive-space pass on the DC-10, I get stuck with this portentous trip, and I'm totally paranoid that something will go wrong, and I'll be stranded in the western Pacific forever."

"Which is quite likely," Duncan said, "given that we're leaving without a mechanic."

Our first stop was Truk, an hour-and-a-half flight from Guam. One of my responsibilities as second officer was to get the local weather information.

"Truk, Truk, Truk," I called on the radio. "Hemisphere five-four-six, requesting weather."

"Go ahead," Truk answered faintly on my fifteenth call.

"Weather!" I shouted. "We need the weather!"

"Stand by," Truk said. "We'll go outside and see." Truk operated on island time, which meant that although our station agents knew exactly when we'd be arriving and that we'd need weather information in order to land, they didn't bother to make the observation until we requested it.

"Gotta love it out here," Neil said, closing the skiing magazine he'd been perusing and starting a descent. "Straight lines between destinations, no crossing or speed restrictions, no air traffic control badgering you every two minutes, no snow or ice . . . this is what I call stress-free flying." Stress-free for him, maybe. He wasn't trying to get home.

"Hemisphere five-four-six, Truk," I heard in my headphones.

"Go ahead," I responded.

"Da weather is good."

I sighed and asked if they had a current altimeter setting. Once I got to Newark (*if* I got to Newark), I'd only be flying in and out of airports with professionally delivered, accurate, and relevant weather information. No more playing twenty questions.

"Two-niner-niner-four."

"Is there any wind?" Since Truk didn't have a control tower, we had to choose which way to land based on the wind direction as reported by the agent.

"No."

"Is it raining?" Fortunately, we didn't have to worry about smog, haze, or fog. The only thing that could restrict our visibility was rain.

"No rain."

"Thank you," I said. "We'll be there in seven minutes."

"Okay," Truk said. "You have some wild pigs."

"Say again?" Sometimes it was hard to understand the local accents.

"There are wild pigs on da runway."

"Wild pigs?" I asked.

"Yes."

"How *many* wild pigs?"

"A few."

"What part of the runway?"

"Da middle."

"Do you think someone could go out there and encourage them to move?" I suggested.

"Already tried. Dey don't want to move."

I filled out the landing data form and passed it to Neil. "There seem to be wild pigs on the runway," I said.

"Wild pigs?" he asked. "What does that mean?"

"It means we should overfly the runway and take a look," Duncan said, scratching his armpit and then sniffing his hand.

Neil assented, and I told Truk our plans, then made an announcement on the PA explaining to the passengers what we'd be doing.

When we flew over the runway, and sure enough, there was a group of pigs sitting on the tarmac.

"Bummer," Neil said, looking uncertain.

"Try buzzing them off," Duncan suggested.

Neil descended to five hundred feet and roared across the runway. The pigs didn't move.

"I thought pigs were supposed to be smart," he said.

"They are smart," Duncan said. "They know precisely where to sit to block the runway."

I put my head in my hands.

On our third pass, one of the pigs got up and sauntered over to the grass alongside the taxiway. The others followed.

We touched down softly on the numbers, and Neil put the throttles into reverse, called for Duncan to extend the spoilers, and gently pumped the brakes.

One landing down, five to go, I thought to myself.

Suddenly, there was a thud, and the airplane lurched to the left.

"What was that?" Neil asked, struggling to get the airplane back under control.

"Too bad we don't have a mechanic on board," Duncan said, "or we might have a chance of fixing whatever it was."

"It could be nothing," Neil said.

"Then again," Duncan said, "it could be substantial."

After Neil shut down the engines, I left the cockpit to open the cargo door. The front half of the Atoll Local airplane (where the first fifteen rows of seats would normally have been) was a cargo area. The top of the fuselage opened by means of an electric switch, and baggage handlers rode up on a forklift to load and unload appropriate cargo.

"You got one!" a baggage handler said, jumping off the forklift into the airplane. He was barefoot and his teeth were stained red from chewing betel nut.

"Got what?" I asked.

"One of dem pigs," he said, grinning. He flattened his right hand to make it seem like an airplane landing, and crashed it into his left hand. "Boom! Dem other pigs run away fast! They don't want to go *boom* like their brother!" He began throwing boxes onto the forklift.

Although it was my job to conduct the walk-around inspection before each takeoff, Neil and Duncan came with me. Without a mechanic, we'd have to assess the damage ourselves and determine whether the airplane was airworthy.

The tail section looked fine. So did the right wing, the right tires, the nose, and the nosewheel. But the left side looked like it had been through a war. Blood, guts, and fur were splattered over the tires, wheel strut, and leading edge of the wing.

"I could have sworn the runway was clear," Neil said, turning away and running his hands through his hair. "Are these pigs here all the time? Because it's a safety hazard. I'm going to take it up with the chief pilot! This isn't my fault!"

"Nobody's blaming you, Neil," Duncan said. "Everyone knows the Atoll Local is cursed. If it hadn't been pigs, it would have been something else."

I took several deep breaths and tried to ignore everything except the structure of the airplane. The tires were still inflated and appeared undamaged. There weren't any new dents or leaks or dangling parts.

"I think the airplane's okay," I said.

Neil nodded in agreement.

"Is it possible the curse of the Atoll Local has been lifted?" Duncan asked, kicking at bits of fur on the tires. "Is it possible we escaped the jaws of death unscathed? Could Lady Luck be smiling down upon us?"

In Pohnpei, the next stop, we almost ran off the runway.

It was a short runway to begin with, ending abruptly at the water's edge, and when the wind, which had been reported as a headwind, shifted to a tailwind just as we touched down, I knew we were in trouble. Even with Duncan and Neil both standing on the brakes, the airplane kept rolling.

I smelled a new wave of Duncan's sweat and noticed dark roots in Neil's otherwise perfect blond hair. I thought about the splash we'd make when we hit the water and wondered if we'd sink or float.

But at the very end of the runway the airplane stopped. The three of us caught our breaths while watching waves breaking on the rocks just beyond the nosewheel.

"The curse is upon us," Duncan whispered.

"Shut up, Duncan!" I said.

"Shit happens," Neil said, turning the airplane around and taxiing toward the ramp.

"And more shit happens on the Atoll Local than any other flight," Duncan added.

I rushed through my walk-around, noting with relief that most of the pig parts had blown off. The fewer passengers who saw blood and guts on the airplane, the better. If the fueler hurried, we could be in the air in ten minutes and maybe make up some of the time we'd lost waiting for the mechanic in Guam and buzzing the runway in Truk.

I arrived in the cockpit to find Paulina, one of our two flight attendants, sitting in the jump seat crying. Paulina was a relatively new flight attendant, and this was her first Atoll Local.

"This trip is cursed," she cried. "First we killed a pig, then we almost crashed into the ocean."

"Now, Paulina, honey," Neil began, handing her his handkerchief. "How can a trip be cursed?"

"I want to get off before something worse happens," Paulina said, blowing her nose.

"Hitting the pig was an accident," Neil said. "It had nothing to do with a curse."

Duncan snorted.

"And if you get off, we'll *all* be stuck here," Neil continued. "There's no one to replace you, and we're not allowed to take off unless we have two flight attendants."

I put my head down on the desk. I was never going to get to Newark.

"I know I'll lose my job," Paulina said, stroking her uniform skirt, "but I just have this feeling . . ."

"You need to transcend your emotions," Neil said, putting his arm around her. "You're a professional. You have responsibilities."

"I know," she said, resting her head against Neil's shoulder. "But when my boyfriend heard all the things that happened—"

"How does your boyfriend know what happened?" Duncan interrupted.

"He lives here on Pohnpei," she said. "He came to the airport to see me. He's waiting over there by the fence." She pointed out the window.

I looked up from the desk and rolled my eyes at Duncan.

"Maybe Neil could go talk to your boyfriend and try explaining the situation," Duncan suggested, looking pointedly at Neil.

"Would that be okay, Paulina, honey?" Neil asked.

"Well," she said, drying her eyes with the handkerchief. "I guess."

"Wait right here," Neil said, standing up.

The three of us watched out the window while Neil engaged in animated conversation with a burly young Pohnpei native dressed in shorts and a T-shirt. Twenty minutes later, Neil returned to the cockpit with Paulina's boyfriend. The boyfriend had never been on an airplane and was in awe of all the switches and instruments. Neil invited him to sit in the left seat and play with the control wheel, all the while explaining the importance of Paulina's job. Eventually the boyfriend kissed Paulina, asked her to buy him some souvenirs in Hawaii, and exited down the aft airstairs.

By the time we landed at Bucholz Army Air Field on Kwajalein Atoll, we were already running two hours late.

"We have a stretcher patient for you," the agent announced, entering the cockpit.

"If we had a mechanic, we could take a stretcher patient," Duncan said. "But we don't have a mechanic, so we can't take a stretcher patient." The Atoll Local was the only airplane equipped to handle stretcher patients. There was a special kit in the cargo compartment that could convert six passenger seats into space for a stretcher. *If* a mechanic was available to install it.

"I thought we were supposed to be informed of all stretcher patients before takeoff from Guam," Neil said.

"It just happened," the agent said. "The guy fell off a roof. He has head and internal injuries. He needs to get to Honolulu as soon as possible."

"Bummer," Neil said.

"Maybe we could call operations in Guam and try to find out about this stretcher kit," Duncan said. "If they can give us instructions, we can probably put it together."

∞

It took Neil, Duncan, and me almost an hour to put together the stretcher kit. By the time we took off for Majuro we were a full three hours behind schedule, and I'd given up making my connection.

"Are we having fun yet?" Neil asked, leveling off at cruising altitude.

"Not especially," Duncan said. "However, I didn't pick up this trip to have fun, so I'm not disappointed."

"You *picked up* this trip?" I asked in surprise. Picking up a trip meant volunteering for it.

"I've flown nine hundred and seventy-one hours so far this year," Duncan said. "An Atoll Local is worth about twenty hours—more if things go wrong. After this trip I only need to fly one more before I get two months of paid vacation." Airline pilots were not allowed to fly more than one thousand hours in any calendar year. Since it was only October, Duncan wouldn't be legal to fly again until January 1.

"How did you sneak that one past scheduling?" Neil asked.

"They know about it," Duncan said. "But there's nothing they can do because they're chronically understaffed out here."

There was a knock on the cockpit door, and Milli, the other flight attendant, let herself in.

"We have a little problem," she began.

"Sit down and relax," Neil said, pointing to the jump seat. "It can't be that bad."

"It's pretty bad," she said, sitting down. "Did you happen to notice those twenty Mormon missionaries we picked up in Pohnpei?"

"Let me think," Neil said. "Do you mean those shorthaired twenty-year-olds wearing dark pants, white shirts, blue ties, and pins saying Elder so-and-so?" He smiled at Milli.

Milli didn't smile back. "It seems they'd just come from some sort of fiesta where there was a lot of local food," she said. "Now they all have violent diarrhea. They're fighting over the bathrooms, and some of them couldn't wait and had to use the airsickness bags. It's bad back there, believe me."

"Do we have any doctors on board?" Duncan asked.

"Just the nurse who came with the stretcher patient," Milli said. "She says they need medical attention."

"What do you think we should do?" Neil asked.

"Radio ahead to Majuro," Duncan said. "Just when we thought things couldn't get any worse . . ."

When we landed in Majuro, Hemisphere's station agent told us the doctor was on his way from the mission village, twenty miles away. In the meantime we were to get all the sick passengers off the airplane and into the shade.

Most of the missionaries were too weak to walk, and they had to be driven on the forklift the hundred yards from the airplane to the shady area beside the terminal (the terminal itself was not air-conditioned and didn't have seating). There they lay on the ground moaning and clutching their stomachs for an hour until the doctor arrived. He gave each of them a shot, told the flight attendants to make sure they drank at least two ounces of liquid an hour, and said they could get back on the plane.

"They're too sick to fly," Neil said, turning away in revulsion. "We can't transport them in this condition."

"Look," the doctor said. "The best place for them is a hospital in Hawaii. The shots I administered will stop the cramps and diarrhea and probably put them to sleep."

"We won't get to Honolulu for another six hours," Neil said. "Will the shots last that long?"

"Hopefully," the doctor said.

We lifted off from Majuro five hours later than scheduled. One more stop, I told myself. Please don't let anything else happen, I appealed to a higher power. Please let me get to Honolulu and then onto the eleven-hour nonstop to Newark.

"I hate to bring up an unpleasant subject," Duncan began. "But we need to consider the issue of duty time."

"Isn't it something like seventeen and a half hours for international trips?" Neil asked. The Hemisphere company manual permitted pilots flying international trips to be on duty for a maximum of seventeen and a half hours between rest periods. If, before takeoff, it appeared that by completing the next flight segment a cockpit crew would exceed seventeen and a half hours on duty, they would have to be taken off the flight until they'd received the required amount of rest.

"We reported to the airport at noon, Guam time," Duncan said. "It's now three A.M., Guam time. We have another hour and a half before Johnston, then a two-hour-and-forty-five-minute flight to Honolulu. According to my calculations, if we spend any more than fifteen minutes on the ground in Johnston, we'll be taking off without enough duty time to reach Honolulu."

"No problem," Neil said, pushing the throttles forward to maximum cruise speed. "We'll fly faster."

"Neil," Duncan said. "I know you're an optimistic kind of guy, but I think you should prepare yourself for the worst."

The worst would be having to spend twelve hours on Johnston Atoll, the only runway between Majuro and Hawaii. Johnston was a little over a mile square and resembled an aircraft carrier. The runway ran the entire length of the island, and barracks lined both sides. The military used Johnston to dispose of nerve gas, and every resident carried around a gas mask just in case there was a leak.

"Johnston isn't answering the radio," I announced, fifty miles out. Johnston, being a military installation, was usually prompt in responding. They would deliver accurate weather and relay the number of passengers and weight of the baggage so I could compute the weight and balance for departure. Having the weight and balance completed in advance could save a good ten minutes on the ground. And if we were going to make a fifteen-minute turn, we would need every possible advantage.

"Keep trying," Neil said.

"Maybe the agent went to the bathroom or something," I suggested, wishfully.

"It's more likely there was a gas leak and everyone's dead," Duncan said.

"Let's keep focused on the positive side," Neil said.

"I wish there was a positive side to look at," Duncan said.

Me, too, I thought, continuing to try to reach Johnston as we descended. But there was no reply, and we had only two hours of fuel left, the required amount to hold overhead should Johnston experience a gas leak (supposedly they could clean up anything within two hours).

"I think I should call Guam on the HF," I said. At certain times of the day, on certain frequencies, under certain meteorological conditions, the high frequency radio was capable of reaching Guam operations. "They can get Johnston on the phone and relay the weather to us."

"Lots of luck," Duncan said.

"It's worth a try," Neil said.

On the first three frequencies I tried I heard only static. But on the fourth Guam answered loud and clear.

"Can you call and tell them we'll be there in ten minutes?" I asked. "We're having trouble reaching them on the radio."

"Why are you going to Johnston?" the dispatcher asked—the very same dispatcher who'd sentenced me to this trip in the first place.

Because it was part of your charming *gift*, I wanted to tell him.

"Because it's on our flight plan," I said instead. The Atoll Local always stopped on Johnston.

"You don't have any passengers out of Johnston," the dispatcher said. "You should have picked up a new flight plan in Majuro." I turned on the speaker so Duncan and Neil could hear.

"I never saw a new flight plan," Neil said, looking through the paperwork from Majuro.

"The mysterious disappearing flight plan," Duncan said, humming the theme song from "The Twilight Zone."

"What do we do now?" Neil asked.

"Tell them that since we never received a new flight plan we have to land in Johnston for fuel," Duncan said.

I told Guam to call Johnston and tell them we needed fuel. In the meantime we'd circle overhead.

"Johnston doesn't answer any of the phone numbers we have for them," the dispatcher said. "They're probably asleep."

"I guess we're going to have to wake them up," Duncan said.

"How?" Neil asked.

"Buzz their barracks," Duncan said.

It took only one pass before the runway lights came on and an irate colonel got on the radio demanding to know what the hell we thought we were doing.

"Sorry about waking you up," Neil said. "But there was a misunderstanding, and we're going to need some fuel."

Circling over Johnston had cost us twenty minutes. Waiting for the fueler to be roused and driven to the ramp took another fifteen minutes. By the time we were ready for takeoff, we had only an hour and a half of legal duty time left.

"Bummer," Neil said. "This doesn't look like the kind of place where we want to spend twelve hours." I was doomed. I would never get away from these islands.

Duncan looked out the window and pondered the barren landscape. "The way I see it," he finally said, "we have a medical emergency. If we don't get the missionaries and the guy who fell off the roof to Honolulu, they might all die. So even if we do exceed our legal duty time by an hour or so, we're doing it for humanitarian reasons. I don't see how they could punish us, given the circumstances."

"I can live with that," Neil said.

I breathed a huge sigh of relief.

When we took off again it was daylight, and I was starting to believe we might actually make it to Hawaii. Of course, I had long ago missed all of Hemisphere's connecting flights to the mainland, but I might be able to hitch a ride on another airline. From Honolulu there would be a lot of possibilities.

"Either of you ever spent any time in a tank?" Neil asked, leveling off at thirty-three thousand feet.

"A tank?" Duncan asked.

"A sensory deprivation tank," Neil said. "I think you'd really benefit from half an hour once a week. I used to be strung tight as a wire until I started tanking. In the beginning I went after every flight. Now I just go once a month for stress management."

"I hate baths," Duncan said, inserting his right index finger into his ear. "You just soak in your own dirt." He removed his finger and examined it.

"You take a shower first," Neil said. "You should really try it."

"It's not my kind of thing," Duncan said.

"How about you, Kendra?" Neil asked. "Have you ever tried tanking?"

"No," I answered, starting to laugh at the absurdity of the conversation. There we were, running six hours late. We'd hit a pig and almost run off a runway. We had one critically injured passenger and twenty with diarrhea. We'd been on duty for eighteen hours and awake for almost twenty-four. And Neil was talking about sensory deprivation tanks. I understand why Duncan called it the Atoll *Loco!*

"You could use a few hours a week," Neil said. "I've never met anyone so tense."

"I'll be fine once we get to Hawaii," I said.

"*If* we get to Hawaii," Duncan added. "There are still a million ways for the curse to manifest itself."

"Don't you dare jinx us again," I warned, reaching for the pitcher of ice water the flight attendants replenished every few hours.

"We could lose an engine. Experience an explosive decompression. Have a cabin fire or a hydraulic failure," Duncan began.

"Can't you be quiet for one more hour?" I pleaded. "We're almost there—"

"We could be hijacked," Duncan continued. "We could have a fuel leak—"

"I can't take any more," I said, laughing uncontrollably. "If you say one more word, you're going to get wet." I held the pitcher above his head.

"We could have a loss of all generators," he persisted. "There could be an electrical fire. We could have a cracked window—"

I poured some of the water on his head, laughing so hard I thought my side would split open.

Duncan grabbed the pitcher and splashed water on me.

"Let's chill, okay?" Neil said.

Duncan poured some water on Neil's head.

Neil turned bright red, and I had a sinking feeling we'd gone too far. But then he started to laugh. There was a can of 7Up on the instrument panel, and he shook it up. He aimed it at Duncan and pulled off the top. Soda covered all of us.

We were laughing so hard we didn't hear Paulina enter the cockpit, but we did hear her scream. That made us laugh even harder.

"You've all gone crazy!" she yelled, backing out. "We're going to crash and die!"

"Come back," Neil called. "We're just having a water fight." He shook up another can of 7Up and drenched us all again.

The interphone rang, and I picked it up.

"What's going on up there?" Milli asked. "I've got twenty-one medical emergencies, and now Paulina is crying in the galley, saying we're all going to die. Can I get a little reassurance, please?"

"Everything's fine," I said, choking back hysterics. "I can't imagine what she's talking about."

And, suddenly, everything was fine. We were going to get to Honolulu, and I was going to make it to Boston. Within a few months I would be upgrading to first officer, and it wouldn't be long before I was making takeoffs and landings again. Takeoffs and landings in an airline jet. The goal I'd set out to achieve. I couldn't wait!

By the time Diamond Head came into sight, we'd cleaned up the cockpit and dried off as well as we could. We all had wet, sticky hair, but we were too tired to care. Duncan and Neil had hats to wear, and as soon as I cleared customs, I was going down to the crew room to shower and change.

"Are all Atoll Locals like this one?" Neil asked as we taxied to the gate.

"Atoll Locals are just like any other kind of flying," Duncan said. "Boring in the back, crazy in the cockpit."

RANDY BLUME IS AN

EXPERIENCED PILOT AND

FLIGHT INSTRUCTOR WHO HAS

FLOWN FOR CHARTER, FREIGHT,

COMMUTER, REGIONAL, AND

MAJOR AIRLINES. SHE LIVES IN

MASSACHUSETTS WITH HER SON.